"The Second World War was over—and there I was at high noon, crossing Times Square with a Purple Heart on."
—ELIOT ROSEWATER
PRESIDENT, The Rosewater Foundation

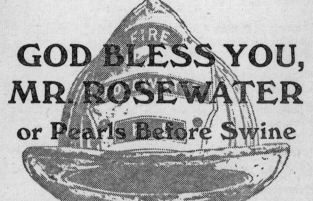

GOD BLESS YOU,
MR. ROSEWATER

or Pearls Before Swine

KURT VONNEGUT, JR.

A Dell Book

For Alvin Davis, the telepath,
the hoodlums' friend

Published by
DELL PUBLISHING CO., INC.
1 Dag Hammarskjold Plaza
New York, N.Y. 10017

Reprinted by arrangement with Delacorte Press
A Seymour Lawrence book, New York, N.Y. 10017

Printed in the U.S.A.
Previous Dell Edition #2929
New Dell Edition
First printing—January 1970
Second printing—March 1970
Third printing—April 1970
Fourth printing—May 1970
Fifth printing—November 1970
Sixth printing—February 1971
Seventh printing—April 1971
Eighth printing—August 1971
Ninth printing—October 1971
Tenth printing—February 1972
Eleventh printing—May 1972
Twelfth printing—July 1972
Thirteenth printing—August 1972
Fourteenth printing—October 1972
Fifteenth printing—March 1973
Sixteenth printing—June 1973
Seventeenth printing—July 1973
Eighteenth printing—September 1973
Nineteenth printing—October 1973
Twentieth printing—November 1973
Twenty-first printing—February 1974
Twenty-second printing—May 1974

1.

A SUM OF MONEY is a leading character in this tale
about people, just as a sum of honey might properly
be a leading character in a tale about bees.

The sum was $87,472,033.61 on June 1, 1964, to pick
a day. That was the day it caught the soft eyes of a boy
shyster named Norman Mushari. The income the
interesting sum produced was $3,500,000 a year, nearly
$10,000 a day—Sundays, too.

The sum was made the core of a charitable and
cultural foundation in 1947, when Norman Mushari
was only six. Before that, it was the fourteenth largest
family fortune in America, the Rosewater fortune. It was
stashed into a foundation in order that tax-collectors
and other predators not named Rosewater might be
prevented from getting their hands on it. And the baroque
masterpiece of legal folderol that was the charter of the
Rosewater Foundation declared, in effect, that the
presidency of the Foundation was to be inherited in the
same manner as the British Crown. It was to be handed
down throughout all eternity to the closest and oldest
heirs of the Foundation's creator, Senator Lister Ames
Rosewater of Indiana.

Siblings of the President were to become officers of
the Foundation upon reaching the age of twenty-one.

All officers were officers for life, unless proved legally
insane. They were free to compensate themselves for
their services as lavishly as they pleased, but only from
the Foundation's income.

R

As required by law, the charter prohibited the Senator's
heirs having anything to do with the management of
the Foundation's capital. Caring for the capital became
the responsibility of a corporation that was born
simultaneously with the Foundation. It was called,
straightforwardly enough, The Rosewater Corporation.
Like almost all corporations, it was dedicated to prudence
and profit, to balance sheets. Its employees were very
well paid. They were cunning and happy and energetic
on that account. Their main enterprise was the churning
of stocks and bonds of other corporations. A minor
activity was the management of a saw factory, a bowling
alley, a motel, a bank, a brewery, extensive farms in
Rosewater County, Indiana, and some coal mines in
northern Kentucky.

The Rosewater Corporation occupied two floors at 500
Fifth Avenue, in New York, and maintained small branch
offices in London, Tokyo, Buenos Aires and Rosewater
County. No member of the Rosewater Foundation could
tell the Corporation what to do with the capital.
Conversely, the Corporation was powerless to tell the
Foundation what to do with the copious profits the
Corporation made.

R

These facts became known to young Norman Mushari
when, upon graduating from Cornell Law School at the
top of his class, he went to work for the Washington,
D.C., law firm that had designed both the Foundation
and the Corporation, the firm of McAllister, Robjent,

Reed and McGee. He was of Lebanese extraction, the
son of a Brooklyn rug merchant. He was five feet and
three inches tall. He had an enormous ass, which was
luminous when bare.

He was the youngest, the shortest, and by all odds the
least Anglo-Saxon male employee in the firm. He was
put to work under the most senile partner, Thurmond
McAllister, a sweet old poop who was seventy-six. He
would never have been hired if the other partners hadn't
felt that McAllister's operations could do with just a
touch more viciousness.

No one ever went out to lunch with Mushari. He took
nourishment alone in cheap cafeterias, and plotted the
violent overthrow of the Rosewater Foundation. He knew
no Rosewaters. What engaged his emotions was the fact
that the Rosewater fortune was the largest single money
package represented by McAllister, Robjent, Reed and
McGee. He recalled what his favorite professor, Leonard
Leech, once told him about getting ahead in law. Leech
said that, just as a good airplane pilot should always be
looking for places to land, so should a lawyer be looking
for situations where large amounts of money were about
to change hands.

"In every big transaction," said Leech, "there is a
magic moment during which a man has surrendered a
treasure, and during which the man who is due to receive
it has not yet done so. An alert lawyer will make that
moment his own, possessing the treasure for a magic
microsecond, taking a little of it, passing it on. If the
man who is to receive the treasure is unused to wealth,
has an inferiority complex and shapeless feelings of guilt,
as most people do, the lawyer can often take as much
as half the bundle, and still receive the recipient's
blubbering thanks."

The more Mushari rifled the firm's confidential files
relative to the Rosewater Foundation, the more excited
he became. Especially thrilling to him was that part of
the charter which called for the immediate expulsion of

any officer adjudged insane. It was common gossip in the office that the very first president of the Foundation, Eliot Rosewater, the Senator's son, was a lunatic. This characterization was a somewhat playful one, but as Mushari knew, playfulness was impossible to explain in a court of law. Eliot was spoken of by Mushari's co-workers variously as "The Nut," "The Saint," "The Holy Roller," "John the Baptist," and so on.

"By all means," Mushari mooned to himself, "we must get this specimen before a judge."

From all reports, the person next in line to be President of the Foundation, a cousin in Rhode Island, was inferior in all respects. When the magic moment came, Mushari would represent him.

Mushari, being tone-deaf, did not know that he himself had an office nickname. It was contained in a tune that someone was generally whistling when he came or went. The tune was "Pop Goes the Weasel."

R

Eliot Rosewater became President of the Foundation in 1947. When Mushari began to investigate him seventeen years later, Eliot was forty-six. Mushari, who thought of himself as brave little David about to slay Goliath, was exactly half his age. And it was almost as though God Himself wanted little David to win, for confidential document after document proved that Eliot was crazy as a loon.

In a locked file inside the firm's vault, for instance, was an envelope with three seals on it—and it was supposed to be delivered unopened to whomever took over the Foundation when Eliot was dead.

Inside was a letter from Eliot, and this is what it said:

Dear Cousin, or whoever you may be—
    Congratulations on your great good fortune.
Have fun. It may increase your perspective to know

what sorts of manipulators and custodians your unbelievable wealth has had up to now.

Like so many great American fortunes, the Rosewater pile was accumulated in the beginning by a humorless, constipated Christian farm boy turned speculator and briber during and after the Civil War. The farm boy was Noah Rosewater, my great-grandfather, who was born in Rosewater County, Indiana.

Noah and his brother George inherited from their pioneer father six hundred acres of farmland, land as dark and rich as chocolate cake, and a small saw factory that was nearly bankrupt. War came.

George raised a rifle company, marched away at its head.

Noah hired a village idiot to fight in his place, converted the saw factory to the manufacture of swords and bayonets, converted the farm to the raising of hogs. Abraham Lincoln declared that no amount of money was too much to pay for the restoration of the Union, so Noah priced his merchandise in scale with the national tragedy. And he made this discovery: Government objections to the price or quality of his wares could be vaporized with bribes that were pitifully small.

He married Cleota Herrick, the ugliest woman in Indiana, because she had four hundred thousand dollars. With her money he expanded the factory and bought more farms, all in Rosewater County. He became the largest individual hog farmer in the North. And, in order not to be victimized by meat packers, he bought controlling interest in an Indianapolis slaughterhouse. In order not to be victimized by steel suppliers, he bought controlling interest in a steel company in Pittsburgh. In order not to be victimized by coal suppliers, he bought controlling interest in several mines. In order not

to be victimized by money lenders, he founded
a bank.

And his paranoid reluctance to be a victim
caused him to deal more and more in valuable
papers, in stocks and bonds, and less and less in
swords and pork. Small experiments with worthless
papers convinced him that such papers could be
sold effortlessly. While he continued to bribe
persons in government to hand over treasuries and
national resources, his first enthusiasm became the
peddling of watered stock.

When the United States of America, which was
meant to be a Utopia for all, was less than a
century old, Noah Rosewater and a few men like
him demonstrated the folly of the Founding Fathers
in one respect: those sadly recent ancestors had
not made it the law of the Utopia that the wealth
of each citizen should be limited. This oversight
was engendered by a weak-kneed sympathy for
those who loved expensive things, and by the
feeling that the continent was so vast and valuable,
and the population so thin and enterprising, that
no thief, no matter how fast he stole, could more
than mildly inconvenience anyone.

Noah and a few like him perceived that the
continent was in fact finite, and that venal office-
holders, legislators in particular, could be persuaded
to toss up great hunks of it for grabs, and to toss
them in such a way as to have them land where
Noah and his kind were standing.

Thus did a handful of rapacious citizens come
to control all that was worth controlling in
America. Thus was the savage and stupid and
entirely inappropriate and unnecessary and
humorless American class system created. Honest,
industrious, peaceful citizens were classed as
bloodsuckers, if they asked to be paid a living
wage. And they saw that praise was reserved

henceforth for those who devised means of getting
paid enormously for commiting crimes against
which no laws had been passed. Thus the American
dream turned belly up, turned green, bobbed to
the scummy surface of cupidity unlimited, filled
with gas, went *bang* in the noonday sun.

E pluribus unum is surely an ironic motto to
inscribe on the currency of this Utopia gone bust,
for every grotesquely rich American represents
property, privileges, and pleasures that have been
denied the many. An even more instructive motto,
in the light of history made by the Noah
Rosewaters, might be: *Grab much too much, or
you'll get nothing at all.*

And Noah begat Samuel, who married Geraldine
Ames Rockefeller. Samuel became even more
interested in politics than his father had been,
served the Republican Party tirelessly as a
king-maker, caused that party to nominate men
who would whirl like dervishes, bawl fluent
Babylonian, and order the militia to fire into crowds
whenever a poor man seemed on the point of
suggesting that he and a Rosewater were equal
in the eyes of the law.

And Samuel bought newspapers, and preachers,
too. He gave them this simple lesson to teach, and
they taught it well: *Anybody who thought that
the United States of America was supposed to be a
Utopia was a piggy, lazy, God-damned fool.*
Samuel thundered that no American factory hand
was worth more than eighty cents a day. And
yet he could be thankful for the opportunity to pay
a hundred thousand dollars or more for a painting
by an Italian three centuries dead. And he capped
this insult by giving paintings to museums for the
spiritual elevation of the poor. The museums were
closed on Sundays.

And Samuel begat Lister Ames Rosewater, who

married Eunice Eliot Morgan. There was something to be said for Lister and Eunice: unlike Noah and Cleota and Samuel and Geraldine, they could laugh as though they meant it. As a curious footnote to history, Eunice became Woman's Chess Champion of the United States in 1927, and again in 1933.

Eunice also wrote an historical novel about a female gladiator, *Ramba of Macedon,* which was a best-seller in 1936. Eunice died in 1937, in a sailing accident in Cotuit, Massachusetts. She was a wise and amusing person, with very sincere anxieties about the condition of the poor. She was my mother.

Her husband, Lister, never was in business. From the moment of his birth to the time I am writing this, he has left the manipulation of his assets to lawyers and banks. He has spent nearly the whole of his adult life in the Congress of the United States, teaching morals, first as a Representative from the district whose heart is Rosewater County, and then as Senator from Indiana. That he is or ever was an Indiana person is a tenuous political fiction. And Lister begat Eliot.

Lister has thought about the effects and implications of his inherited wealth about as much as most men think about their left big toes. The fortune has never amused, worried, or tempted him. Giving ninety-five per cent of it to the Foundation you now control didn't cause him a twinge.

And Eliot married Sylvia DuVrais Zetterling, a Parisienne beauty who came to hate him. Her mother was a patroness of painters. Her father was the greatest living cellist. Her maternal grandparents were a Rothschild and a DuPont.

And Eliot became a drunkard, a Utopian dreamer, a tinhorn saint, an aimless fool.

Begat he not a soul.

Bon voyage, dear Cousin or whoever you are. Be generous. Be kind. You can safely ignore the arts and sciences. They never helped anybody. Be a sincere, attentive friend of the poor.

The letter was signed,

The late Eliot Rosewater.

His heart going like a burglar alarm, Norman Mushari hired a large safe-deposit box, and he put the letter into it. That first piece of solid evidence would not be lonesome long.

Mushari went back to his cubicle, reflected that Sylvia was in the process of divorcing Eliot, with old McAllister representing the defendant. She was living in Paris, and Mushari wrote a letter to her, suggesting that it was customary in friendly, civilized divorce actions for litigants to return each other's letters. He asked her to send him any letters from Eliot that she might have saved.

He got fifty-three such letters by return mail.

2.

ELIOT ROSEWATER was born in 1918, in Washington D.C. Like his father, who claimed to represent the Hoosier State, Eliot was raised and educated and entertained on the Eastern Seaboard and in Europe. The family visited the so-called "home" in Rosewater County very briefly every year, just long enough to reinvigorate the lie that it was home.

Eliot had unremarkable academic careers at Loomis and Harvard. He became an expert sailor during summers in Cotuit, on Cape Cod, and an intermediate skier during winter vacations in Switzerland.

He left Harvard Law School on December 8, 1941, to volunteer for the Infantry of the Army of the United States. He served with distinction in many battles. He rose to the rank of captain, was a company commander. Near the end of the war in Europe, Eliot suffered what was diagnosed as combat fatigue. He was hospitalized in Paris, where he wooed and won Sylvia.

After the war, Eliot returned to Harvard with his stunning wife, took his law degree. He went on to specialize in international law, dreamed of helping the United Nations in some way. He received a doctorate in that field, and was handed simultaneously the presidency of the new Rosewater Foundation. His duties, according to the charter, were exactly as flimsy or as formidable as he himself declared them to be.

Eliot chose to take the Foundation seriously. He bought a town house in New York, with a fountain in the foyer. He put a Bentley and a Jaguar in the garage. He hired a suite of offices in the Empire State Building. He had them painted lime, burnt-orange and oyster white. He proclaimed them the headquarters for all the beautiful, compassionate and scientific things he hoped to do.

He was a heavy drinker, but no one worried about it. No amount of booze seemed to make him drunk.

R

From 1947 until 1953, the Rosewater Foundation spent fourteen million dollars. Eliot's benefactions covered the full eleemosynary spectrum from a birth control clinic in Detroit to an El Greco for Tampa, Florida. Rosewater dollars fought cancer and mental illness and race prejudice and police brutality and countless other miseries, encouraged college professors to look for truth, bought beauty at any price.

Ironically, one of the studies Eliot paid for had to do with alcoholism in San Diego. When the report was submitted, Eliot was too drunk to read it. Sylvia had to come down to his office to escort him home. A hundred people saw her trying to lead him across the sidewalk to a waiting cab. And Eliot recited for them a couplet he had spent all morning composing:

> "Many, many good things have I bought!
> Many, many bad things have I fought!"

R

Eliot stayed contritely sober for two days after that, then disappeared for a week. Among other things he crashed a convention of science-fiction writers in a motel in Milford, Pennsylvania. Norman Mushari learned about this episode from a private detective's report that was in the files of McAllister, Robjent, Reed and McGee. Old McAllister had hired the detective to retrace Eliot's steps, to find out if he had done things that might later legally embarrass the Foundation.

The report contained Eliot's speech to the writers word-for-word. The meeting, including Eliot's drunken interruption, had been taken down on tape.

"I love you sons of bitches," Eliot said in Milford. "You're all I read any more. You're the only ones who'll talk about the *really* terrific changes going on, the only ones crazy enough to know that life is a space voyage, and not a short one, either, but one that'll last for billions of years. You're the only ones with guts enough to *really* care about the future, who *really* notice what machines do to us, what wars do to us, what cities do to us, what big, simple ideas do to us, what tremendous misunderstandings, mistakes, accidents and catastrophes do to us. You're the only ones zany enough to agonize over time and distances without limit, over mysteries that will never die, over the fact that we are right now determining whether the space voyage for the next billion years or so is going to be Heaven or Hell."

R

Eliot admitted later on that science-fiction writers couldn't write for sour apples, but he declared that it didn't matter. He said they were poets just the same, since they were more sensitive to important changes than anybody who was writing well. "The hell with the talented sparrowfarts who write delicately of one small piece of one mere lifetime, when the issues are galaxies, eons, and trillions of souls yet to be born."

R

"I only wish Kilgore Trout were here," said Eliot, "so I could shake his hand and tell him that he is the greatest writer alive today. I have just been told that he could not come because he could not afford to leave his job! And what job does this society give its greatest prophet?" Eliot choked up, and, for a few moments, he couldn't make himself name Trout's job. "They have made him a stock clerk in a trading stamp redemption center in Hyannis!"

This was true. Trout, the author of eighty-seven paperback books, was a very poor man, and unknown outside the science-fiction field. He was sixty-six years old when Eliot spoke so warmly of him.

"Ten thousand years from now," Eliot predicted boozily, "the names of our generals and presidents will be forgotten, and the only hero of our time still remembered will be the author of *2BRO2B*." This was the title of a book by Trout, a title which, upon examination, turned out to be the famous question posed by Hamlet.

R

Mushari dutifully went looking for a copy of the book for his dossier on Eliot. No reputable bookseller had ever heard of Trout. Mushari made his last try at a smut-dealer's hole in the wall. There, amidst the rawest pornography, he found tattered copies of every book Trout had ever written. *2BRO2B*, which had been published at twenty-five cents, cost him five dollars, which was what *The Kama Sutra of Vitsayana* cost, too.

Mushari glanced through the *Kama Sutra*, the long-suppressed oriental manual on the art and techniques of love, read this:

If a man makes a sort of jelly with the juices
of the fruit cassia fistula and eugenie jambolina
and mixes the powder of the plants soma, veronia
anthelminica, eclipta prostata, lohopa-juihirka, and
applies this mixture to the yoni of a woman with
whom he is about to have intercourse, he will
instantly cease to love her.

Mushari didn't see anything funny in that. He never
saw anything funny in anything, so deeply immured
was he by the utterly unplayful spirit of the law.

And he was witless enough, too, to imagine that
Trout's books were very dirty books, since they were
sold for such high prices to such queer people in such
a place. He didn't understand that what Trout had in
common with pornography wasn't sex but fantasies of
an impossibly hospitable world.

R

So Mushari felt swindled as he wallowed through
the garish prose, lusted for sex, learned instead about
automation. Trout's favorite formula was to describe a
perfectly hideous society, not unlike his own, and then,
toward the end, to suggest ways in which it could be
improved. In *2BRO2B* he hypothecated an America in
which almost all of the work was done by machines, and
the only people who could get work had three or more
Ph.D's. There was a serious overpopulation problem, too.

All serious diseases had been conquered. So death
was voluntary, and the government, to encourage
volunteers for death, set up a purple-roofed Ethical
Suicide Parlor at every major intersection, right next
door to an orange-roofed Howard Johnson's. There
were pretty hostesses in the parlor, and Barca-Loungers,
and Muzak, and a choice of fourteen painless ways to
die. The suicide parlors were busy places, because so
many people felt silly and pointless, and because it was

supposed to be an unselfish, patriotic thing to do, to die. The suicides also got free last meals next door.

And so on. Trout had a wonderful imagination.

One of the characters asked a death stewardess if he would go to Heaven, and she told him that of course he would. He asked if he would see God, and she said, "Certainly, honey."

And he said, "I sure hope so. I want to ask Him something I never was able to find out down here."

"What's that?" she said, strapping him in.

"What in hell are people *for*?"

R

In Milford, Eliot told the writers that he wished they would learn more about sex and economics and style, but then he supposed that people dealing with really big issues didn't have much time for such things.

And it occurred to him that a really good science-fiction book had never been written about money. "Just think of the wild ways money is passed around on Earth!" he said. "You don't have to go to the Planet Tralfamadore in Anti-Matter Galaxy 508 G to find weird creatures with unbelievable powers. Look at the powers of an Earthling millionaire! Look at me! I was born naked, just like you, but my God, friends and neighbors, I have thousands of dollars a day to spend!"

He paused to make a very impressive demonstration of his magical powers, writing a smeary check for two hundred dollars for every person there.

"*There's* fantasy for you," he said. "And you go to the bank tomorrow, and it will all come true. It's insane that I should be able to do such a thing, with money so important." He lost his balance for a moment, regained it, and then nearly fell asleep on his feet. He opened his eyes with great effort. "I leave it to you, friends and neighbors, and especially to the immortal Kilgore

Trout: think about the silly ways money gets passed around now, and then think up better ways."

R

Eliot lurched away from Milford, hitchhiked to Swarthmore, Pennsylvania. He went into a small bar there, announced that anyone who could produce a volunteer fireman's badge could drink with him free. He built gradually to a crying jag, during which he claimed to be deeply touched by the idea of an inhabited planet with an atmosphere that was eager to combine violently with almost everything the inhabitants held dear. He was speaking of Earth and the element oxygen.

"When you think about it, boys," he said brokenly, "that's what holds us together more than anything else, except maybe gravity. We few, we happy few, we band of brothers—joined in the serious business of keeping our food, shelter, clothing and loved ones from combining with oxygen. I tell you, boys, I used to belong to a volunteer fire department, and I'd belong to one now, if there were such a human thing, such a *humane* thing, in New York City." This was bunk about Eliot's having been a fireman. The closest he had ever come to that was during his annual childhood visits to Rosewater County, to the family fief. Sycophants among the townies had flattered little Eliot by making him mascot of the Volunteer Fire Department of Rosewater. He had never fought a fire.

"I tell you, boys," he went on, "if those Russian landing barges come barging in some day, and there isn't any way to stop 'em, all the phony bastards who get all the good jobs in this country by kissing ass will be down to meet the conquerers with vodka and caviar, offering to do any kind of work the Russians have in mind. And you know who'll take to the woods with hunting knives and Springfields, who'll go on fighting for a hundred years, by God? The volunteer firemen, that's who."

Eliot was locked up in Swarthmore on a drunk and disorderly charge. When he awoke the next morning, the police called his wife. He apologized to her, slunk home.

R

But he was off again in a month, carousing with firemen in Clover Lick, West Virginia, one night, and in New Egypt, New Jersey, the next. And on that trip he traded clothes with another man, swapped a four-hundred-dollar suit for a 1939 double-breasted blue chalk-stripe, with shoulders like Gibraltar, lapels like the wings of the Archangel Gabriel, and with the creases in the trousers permanently sewed in.

"You must be crazy," said the New Egypt fireman.

"I don't want to look like me," Eliott replied. "I want to look like you. You're the salt of the earth, by God. You're what's good about America, men in suits like that. You're the soul of the U.S. Infantry."

And Eliot eventually traded away everything in his wardrobe but his tails, his dinner jacket, and one gray flannel suit. His sixteen-foot closet became a depressing museums of coveralls, overalls, Robert Hall Easter specials, field jackets, Eisenhower jackets, sweatshirts and so on. Sylvia wanted to burn them, but Eliot told her, "Burn my tails, my dinner jacket and my gray flannel suit instead."

R

Eliot was a flamboyantly sick man, even then, but there was no one to hustle him off for treatment, and no one was as yet entranced by the profits to be made in proving him insane. Little Norman Mushari was only twelve in those troubled days, was assembling plastic model

airplanes, masturbating, and papering his room with
pictures of Senator Joe McCarthy and Roy Cohn. Eliot
Rosewater was the farthest thing from his mind.

Sylvia raised among rich and charming eccentrics,
was too European to have him put away. And the
Senator was in the political fight of his life, rallying the
Republican forces of reaction that had been shattered
by the election of Dwight David Eisenhower. When
told of his son's bizarre way of life, the Senator refused
to worry, on the grounds that the boy was well-bred.
"He's got fiber, he's got spine," the Senator said. "He's
experimenting. He'll come back to his senses any time
he's good and ready. This family never produced and
never will produce a chronic drunk or a chronic
lunatic."

Having said that, he went into the Senate Chamber
to deliver his fairly famous speech on the Golden Age
of Rome, in which he said, in part:

> I should like to speak of the Emperor Octavian,
> of Caesar Augustus, as he came to be known. This
> great humanitarian, and he was a humanitarian
> in the profoundest sense of the word, took
> command of the Roman Empire in a degenerate
> period strikingly like our own. Harlotry, divorce,
> alcoholism, liberalism, homosexuality, pornography,
> abortion, venality, murder, labor racketeering,
> juvenile delinquency, cowardice, atheism, extortion,
> slander, and theft were the height of fashion.
> Rome was a paradise for gangsters, perverts, and
> the lazy working man, just as America is now.
> As in America now, forces of law and order were
> openly attacked by mobs, children were disobedient,
> had no respect for their parents or their country,
> and no decent woman was safe on any street,
> even at high noon! And cunning, sharp-trading,
> bribing foreigners were in the ascendency
> everywhere. And ground under the heels of the

big city money-changers were the honest farmers,
the backbone of the Roman Army and the Roman
soul.

What could be done? Well, there were soft-
headed liberals then as there are bubble-headed
liberals now, and they said what liberals always
say after they have led a great nation to such a
lawless, self-indulgent, polyglot condition: "Things
have never been better! Look at all the freedom!
Look at all the equality! Look how sexual
hypocrisy has been driven from the scene! Oh
boy! People used to get all knotted up inside when
they thought about rape or fornication. Now they
can do both with glee!"

And what did the terrible, black-spirited,
non-fun-loving conservatives of those happy days
have to say? Well, there weren't many of them
left. They were dying off in ridiculed old age.
And their children had been turned against them
by the liberals, by the purveyors of synthetic
sunshine and moonshine, by the something-for-
nothing political strip-teasers, by the people who
loved everybody, including the barbarians, by
people who loved the barbarians so much they
wanted to open all the gates, have all the soldiers
lay their weapons down, and let the barbarians
come in!

That was the Rome that Caesar Augustus came
home to, after defeating those two sex maniacs,
Antony and Cleopatra, in the great sea battle of
Actium. And don't think I have to re-create the
things he thought when he surveyed the Rome he
was said to rule. Let us take a moment of silence,
and let each think what he will of the stews of
today.

There was a moment of silence, too, about thirty
seconds that seemed to some like a thousand years.

And what methods did Caesar Augustus use to put this disorderly house in order? He did what we are so often told we must never, ever do, what we are told will never, ever work: he wrote morals into law, and he enforced those unenforceable laws with a police force that was cruel and unsmiling. He made it illegal for a Roman to behave like a pig. Do you hear me? It became illegal! And Romans caught acting like pigs were strung up by their thumbs, thrown down wells, fed to lions, and given other experiences that might impress them with the desirability of being more decent and reliable than they were. Did it work? You bet your boots it did! Pigs miraculously disappeared! And what do we call the period that followed this now-unthinkable oppression? Nothing more nor less, friends and neighbors, than "The Golden Age of Rome."

R

Am I suggesting that we follow this gory example? Of course I am. Scarcely a day has passed during which I have not said in one way or another: "Let us force Americans to be as good as they should be." Am I in favor of feeding labor crooks to lions? Well, to give those who get such satisfaction from imagining that I am covered with primordial scales a little twinge of pleasure, let me say, "Yes. Absolutely. This afternoon, if it can be arranged." To disappoint my critics, let me add that I am only fooling. I am not entertained by cruel and unusual punishments, not in the least. I am fascinated by the fact that a carrot and a stick can make a donkey go, and that his Space Age discovery may have some application in the world of human beings.

And so on. The Senator said that the carrot and the stick had been built into the Free Enterprise System, as conceived by the Founding Fathers, but that do-gooders, who thought people shouldn't ever have to struggle for anything, had buggered the logic of the system beyond all recognition.

> In summation: *he said,* I see two alternatives before us. We can write morals into law, and enforce those morals harshly, or we can return to a true Free Enterprise System, which has the sink-or-swim justice of Caesar Augustus built into it. I emphatically favor the latter alternative. We must be hard, for we must become again a nation of swimmers, with the sinkers quietly disposing of themselves. I have spoken of another hard time in ancient history. In case you have forgotten the name of it, I shall refresh your memories: "The Golden Age of Rome," friends and neighbors, "The Golden Age of Rome."

As for friends who might have helped Eliot through his time of troubles: he didn't have any. He drove away his rich friends by telling them that whatever they had was based on dumb luck. He advised his artist friends that the only people who paid any attention to what they did were rich horses' asses with nothing more athletic to do. He asked his scholarly friends, "Who has time to read all the boring crap you write and listen to all the boring things you say?" He alienated his friends in the sciences by thanking them extravagantly for scientific advances he had read about in recent newspapers and magazines, by assuring them, with a perfectly straight face, that life was getting better and better, thanks to scientific thinking.

R

And then Eliot entered psychoanalysis. He swore off drinking, took pride in his appearance again, expressed enthusiasm for the arts and sciences, won back many friends.

Sylvia was never happier. But then, one year after the treatments had begun, she was astonished by a call from the analyst. He was resigning the case because, in his taut Viennese opinion, Eliot was untreatable.

"But you've cured him!"

"If I were a Los Angeles quack, dear lady, I would most demurely agree. However, I am not a Swami. Your husband has the most massively defended neurosis I have ever attempted to treat. What the nature of that neurosis is I can't imagine. In one solid year of work, I have not succeeded in even scratching its armor plate."

"But he always comes home from your office so cheerful!"

"Do you know what we talk about?"

"I thought it better not to ask."

"American history! Here is a very sick man, who, among other things, killed his mother, who has a terrifying tyrant for a father. And what does he talk about when I invite him to let his mind wander where it will? American history."

The statement that Eliot had killed his beloved mother was, in a crude way, true. When he was nineteen, he took his mother for a sail in Cotuit Harbor. He jibed. The slashing boom knocked his mother overboard. Eunice Morgan Rosewater sank like a stone.

"I ask him what he dreams about," the doctor continued, "and he tells me, 'Samuel Gompers, Mark Twain, and Alexander Hamilton.' I ask him if his father ever appears in his dreams, and he says, 'No, but Thorsten Veblen often does.' Mrs. Rosewater, I'm defeated. I resign."

R

Eliot seemed merely amused by the doctor's dismissal. "It's a cure he doesn't understand, so he refuses to admit it's a cure," he said lightly.

That evening, he and Sylvia went to the Metropolitan Opera for the opening of a new staging of *Aïda*. The Rosewater Foundation had paid for the costumes. Eliot looked sleekly marvelous, tall, tailcoated, his big, friendly face pink, and his blue eyes glittering with mental hygiene.

Everything was fine until the last scene of the opera, during which the hero and heroine were placed in an airtight chamber to suffocate. As the doomed pair filled their lungs, Eliot called out to them, "You will last a lot longer, if you don't try to sing." Eliot stood, leaned far out of his box, told the singers, "Maybe you don't know anything about oxygen, but I do. Believe me, you must not sing."

Eliot's face went white and blank. Sylvia plucked at his sleeve. He looked at her dazedly, then permitted her to lead him away as easily as she might have led a toy balloon.

3.

NORMAN MUSHARI learned that, on the night of
Aïda, Eliot disappeared again, jumped out of his
homeward-bound cab at Forty-second Street and Fifth
Avenue.

Ten days later, Sylvia got this letter, which was
written on the stationery of the Elsinore Volunteer Fire
Department, Elsinore, California. The name of the place
set him off on a new line of speculation about himself,
to the effect that he was a lot like Shakespeare's Hamlet.

> Dear Ophelia—
> Elsinore isn't quite what I expected, or maybe
> there's more than one, and I've come to the wrong
> one. The high school football players here call
> themselves "The Fighting Danes." In the
> surrounding towns they're known as "The
> Melancholy Danes." In the past three years they
> have won one game, tied two, and lost twenty-four.
> That's what happens, I guess, when Hamlet goes
> in as quarterback.
> The last thing you said to me before I got out
> of the taxicab was that maybe we should get a
> divorce. I did not realize that life had become

that uncomfortable for you. I do realize that I
am a very slow realizer. I still find it hard to
realize that I am an alcoholic, though even
strangers know this right away.

Maybe I flatter myself when I think that I have
things in common with Hamlet, that I have an
important mission, that I'm temporarily mixed up
about how it should be done. Hamlet had one big
edge on me. His father's ghost told him exactly
what he had to do, while I am operating without
instructions. But from somewhere something is
trying to tell me where to go, what to do there,
and why to do it. Don't worry, I don't hear voices.
But there is this feeling that I have a destiny far
away from the shallow and preposterous posing
that is our life in New York. And I roam.

And I roam.

Young Mushari was disappointed to read that Eliot
did *not* hear voices. But the letter did end on a
definitely cracked note. Eliot described the fire apparatus
of Elsinore, as though Sylvia would be avid for such
details.

They paint their fine engines here with orange and
black stripes, like tigers. Very striking! They use
detergent in their water, so that the water will soak
right through wallboard to get at a fire. That
certainly makes good sense, provided it doesn't
harm the pumps and hoses. They haven't been
using it long enough to really know. I told them
they should write the pump manufacturer and
tell him what they're doing, and they said they
would. They think I am a very big volunteer
fireman from back East. They are wonderful
people. They aren't like the sparrowfarts and
dancing masters who come tapping at the

Rosewater Foundation's door. They're like the
Americans I knew in the war.

Be patient, Ophelia.

Love,
Hamlet.

Eliot went from Elsinore to Vashti, Texas, and was
soon arrested. He wandered up to the Vashti firehouse,
covered with dust, needing a shave. He started talking
to some idlers there about how the government ought
to divide up the wealth of the country equally, instead
of some people having more than they could ever use,
and others having nothing.

He rambled on, said such things as, "You know, I
think the main purpose of the Army, Navy, and Marine
Corps is to get poor Americans into clean, pressed,
unpatched clothes, so rich Americans can stand to look
at them." He mentioned a revolution, too. He thought
there might be one in about twenty years, and he
thought it would be a good one, provided infantry
veterans and volunteer firemen led it.

He was thrown in jail as a suspicious character.
They let him go after a mystifying series of questions
and answers. They made him promise never to come
back to Vashti again.

A week after that, he turned up in New Vienna, Iowa.
He wrote another letter to Sylvia on the stationery of
the fire department there. He called Sylvia *the most
patient woman in the world,*" and he told her that her
long vigil was almost over.

I know now, *he wrote,* where I must go. I am
going there with all possible speed! I will telephone
from there! Perhaps I'll stay there forever. It isn't
clear to me yet what I must do when I get there.
But that will become clear, too, I'm sure. The
scales are falling from my eyes!

Incidentally, I told the fire department here

that they might try putting detergent in their
water, but that they should write the pump
manufacturer first. They like the idea. They're
going to bring it up at the next meeting. I've gone
sixteen hours without a drink! I don't miss the
poison at all! Cheers!

When Sylvia got that letter, she immediately had a
recording device attached to her telephone, another
nice break for Norman Mushari. Sylvia did this because
she thought that Eliot had at last gone irrevocably
bananas. When he called, she wanted to record every
clue as to his whereabouts and conditions, so that she
could have him picked up.

The call come:

"Ophelia??"

"Oh, Eliot, Eliot—where are you, darling?"

"In America—among the rickety sons and grandsons
of the pioneers."

"But where? But where?"

"Absolutely anywhere—in an aluminum and glass
phone booth in a drab little American anywhere, with
American nickels, dimes and quarters scattered on the
little gray shelf before me. There is a message written
with a ballpoint pen on the little gray shelf."

"And what does it say?"

" 'Sheila Taylor is a cock-teaser.' I'm sure it's true."

There was an arrogant *blat* from Eliot's end. "Hark!"
said Eliot. "A Greyhound bus has blatted its Roman
trumpets flatulently outside the bus depot, which is also
a candy store. Lo! One old American responds, comes
tottering out. There is no one to bid him farewell, nor
does he look up and down the street for someone to
wish him well. He carries a brown paper parcel tied
with twine. He is going somewhere, no doubt to die.

"He is taking leave of the only town he's ever
known, the only life he's ever know. But he isn't
thinking about saying goodbye to his universe. His whole

being is intent of not offending the mighty bus driver,
who looks down fumingly from his blue leather throne.
Wupps! Too bad! The old American crawled aboard
in fair shape, but now he can't find his ticket. He finds
it at last, too late, too late. The driver is filled with
rage. He slams the door, starts off with a savage clashing
of gears, blows his horn at an old American woman
crossing the street, rattles the windowpanes. Hate,
hate, hate."

"Eliot—is there a river there?"

"My telephone booth is in the broad valley of an open
sewer called the Ohio. The Ohio is thirty miles to the
south. Carp as big as atomic submarines fatten on the
sludge of the sons and grandsons of the pioneers.
Beyond the river lie the once green hills of Kentucky,
the promised land of Dan'l Boone, now gulched and
gashed by strip mines, some of which are owned by a
charitable and cultural foundation endowed by an
interesting old American family named Rosewater.

"On that side of the river, the Rosewater Foundation's
holdings are somewhat diffuse. On this side, though,
right around my phone booth, for a distance of about
fifteen miles in any direction you care to go, the
Foundation owns almost everything. The Foundation,
however, has left the booming night-crawler business
wide open. Signs on every home proclaim,
'Night-crawlers for Sale.'

"The key industry here, hogs and night-crawlers
aside, is the making of saws. The saw factory is owned
by the Foundation, of course. Because saws are so
important here, the athletes of Noah Rosewater
Memorial High School are known as 'The Fighting
Sawmakers.' Actually, there aren't many sawmakers
left. The saw factory is almost fully automatic now. If
you can work a pinball machine, you can run the
factory, make twelve thousand saws a day.

"A young man, a Fighting Sawmaker about eighteen
years old, is strolling insouciantly past my phone booth

now, wearing the sacred blue and white. He looks dangerous, but he wouldn't harm a soul. His two best subjects in school were Citizenship and Problems in Modern American Democracy, both taught by his basketball coach. He understands that anything violent he might do would not only weaken the Republic, but would ruin his own life, too. There is no work for him in Rosewater. There is damn little work for him anywhere. He often carries birth-control devices in his pocket, which many people find alarming and disgusting. The same people find it alarming and disgusting that the boy's father did *not* use birth-control devices. One more kid rotten-spoiled by postwar abundance, one more princeling with gooseberry eyes. He's meeting his girl now, a girl not much older than fourteen—a five-and-ten-cent-store Cleopatra, a four-letter word.

"Across the street is the firehouse—four trucks, three drunks, sixteen dogs, and one cheerful, sober young man with a can of metal polish."

"Oh, Eliot, Eliot—come home, come home."

"Don't you understand, Sylvia? I *am* home. I know now that this has always been home—the Town of Rosewater, the Township of Rosewater, the County of Rosewater, the State of Indiana."

R

"And what do you intend to *do* there, Eliot?"

"I'm going to *care* about these people."

"That's—that's very nice," said Sylvia bleakly. This was a pale and delicate girl, cultivated, wispy. She played the harpsichord, spoke six languages enchantingly. As a child and young woman, she had met many of the greatest men of her time in her parents' home—Picasso, Schweitzer, Hemingway, Toscanini, Churchhill, de Gaulle. She had never seen Rosewater County, had no idea what a night-crawler was, did not know that land anywhere could be so deathly flat, that people anywhere could be so deathly dull.

"I look at these people, these Americans," Eliot went on, "and I realize that they can't even care about themselves any more—because they have no *use*. The factory, the farms, the mines across the river—they're almost completely automatic now. And America doesn't even need these people for war—not any more. Sylvia—I'm going to be an artist."

"An artist?"

"I'm going to love these discarded Americans, even though they're useless and unattractive. *That* is going to be my work of art."

4.

ROSEWATER COUNTY, the canvas Eliot proposed to
paint with love and understanding, was a rectangle on
which other men—other Rosewaters, mainly—had
already made some bold designs. Eliot's predecessors had
anticipated Mondrian. Half the roads ran east and west
and half the roads ran north and south. Bisecting the
county exactly, and stopping at its borders, was a
stagnant canal fourteen miles long. It was the one dash
of reality added by Eliot's great grandfather to a stock
and bond fantasy of a canal that would join Chicago,
Indianapolis, Rosewater and the Ohio. There were now
bullheads, crappies, redeyes, bluegills, and carp in the
canal. It was to people interested in catching such fish
that night-crawlers were sold.

The ancestors of many of the night-crawler
merchants had been stockholders and bondholders in
the Rosewater Inter-State Ship Canal. When the scheme
failed utterly, some of them lost their farms, which
were bought by Noah Rosewater. A Utopian community
in the southwest corner of the county, New Ambrosia,
invested everything it had in the canal, and lost. They
were Germans, communists and atheists who practiced
group marriage, absolute truthfulness, absolute
cleanliness, and absolute love. They were now scattered

to the winds, like the worthless papers that represented
their equity in the canal. No one was sorry to see them
go. Their one contribution to the county that was still
viable in Eliot's time was their brewery, which had
become the home of Rosewater Golden Lager Ambrosia
Beer. On the label of each can of beer was a picture of
the heaven on earth the New Ambrosians had meant to
build. The dream city had spires. The spires had
lightning-rods. The sky was filled with cherubim.

R

The town of Rosewater was in the dead center of
the county. In the dead center of town was a Parthenon
built of honest red brick, columns and all. Its roof was
green copper. The canal ran through it, and so, in the
bustling past, had the New York Central, Monon, and
Nickel Plate Railroads. When Eliot and Sylvia took up
residence, only the canal and the Monon tracks
remained, and the Monon was bankrupt, and its tracks
were brown.

To the west of the Parthenon was the old Rosewater
Saw Company, red brick, too, green-roofed, too. The
spine of its roof was broken, its windows unglazed. It
was a New Ambrosia for barn swallows and bats. Its
four tower clocks were handless. Its big brass whistle
was choked with nests.

To the east of the Parthenon was the County courthouse,
red brick, too, green-roofed, too. Its tower was
identical with that of the old saw company. Three of
its four clocks still had their hands, but they did not run.
Like an abscess at the base of a dead tooth, a private
business had somehow managed to establish itself in the
cellar of the public building. It had a little red neon
sign. "Bella's Beauty Nook," it said. Bella weighed
three hundred fourteen pounds.

To the east of the courthouse was the Samuel

Rosewater Veterans' Memorial Park. It had a flagpole and an honor roll. The honor roll was a four-by-eight sheet of exterior plywood painted black. It was hung on pipe, sheltered by a gable that was only two inches wide. It had all the names of Rosewater County people who had laid down their lives for their country.

R

The only other masonry structures were the Rosewater Mansion and its carriage house, set on an artificial elevation at the east end of the park and surrounded by a rank of iron spikes, and the Noah Rosewater Memorial High School, home of the Fighting Sawmakers, which bounded the park on the south. To the north of the park was the old Rosewater Opera House, a terrifyingly combustible frame wedding cake which had been converted to a firehouse. All else was shithouses, shacks, alcoholism, ignorance, idiocy and perversion, for all that was healthy and busy and intelligent in Rosewater County shunned the county seat.

The new Rosewater Saw Company, all yellow brick and no windows, was set in a cornfield midway between Rosewater and New Ambrosia. It was served by a gleaming new spur of the New York Central, and by a sizzling double-barreled highway that missed the county seat by eleven miles. Near it were the Rosewater Motel and the Rosewater Bowl-A-Rama, and the great grain elevators and animal pens that were shipping points for fruits of the Rosewater Farms. And the few highly paid agronomists, engineers, brewers, accountants and administrators who did all that needed doing lived in a defensive circle of expensive ranch homes in another cornfield near New Ambrosia, a community named, for no reason whatsoever, "Avondale." All had gas-lit patios framed and terraced with railroad ties from the old Nickel Plate right-of-way.

R

Eliot stood in relation to the clean people of Avondale
as a constitutional monarch. They were employees of
the Rosewater Corporation, and the properties they
managed were owned by the Rosewater Foundation.
Eliot could not tell them what to do—but he was surely
the King, and Avondale knew it.

So, when King Eliot and Queen Sylvia took up
residence in the Rosewater Mansion, they were
showered by figs from Avondale—invitations, visits,
flattering notes and calls. All were deflected. Eliot
required Sylvia to receive all prosperous visitors with
an air of shallow, absent-minded cordiality. Every
Avondale woman left the mansion stiffly, as though, as
Eliot observed gleefully, she had a pickle up her ass.

R

Interestingly, the social-climbing technocrats of
Avondale were able to bear the theory that the
Rosewaters snubbed them because the Rosewaters felt
superior to them. They even enjoyed the theory as
they discussed it again and again. They were avid for
lessons in authentic, upper-class snobbery, and Eliot
and Sylvia seemed to be giving those.

But then the King and Queen got the Rosewater
family crystal, silver and gold out of the dank vaults of
the Rosewater County National Bank, began to throw
lavish banquets for morons, perverts, starvelings and
the unemployed.

They listened tirelessly to the misshapen fears and
dreams of people who, by almost anyone's standards,
would have been better off dead, gave them love and
trifling sums of money. The only social life they had
that was untainted by pity had to do with the
Rosewater Volunteer Fire Department. Eliot arose

quickly to the rank of Fire Lieutenant, and Sylvia was
elected President of the Ladies' Auxiliary. Though
Sylvia had never before touched a bowling ball, she was
made captain of the auxiliary's bowling team, too.

Avondale's clammy respect for the monarchy turned
to incredulous contempt, and then to savagery.
Yahooism, drinking, cuckolding, and self-esteem all
took sharp upturns. The voices of Avondale acquired
the tone of bandsaws cutting galvanized tin when
discussing the King and Queen, as though a tyranny
had been overthrown. Avondale was no longer a
settlement of rising young executives. It was peopled by
vigorous members of the true ruling class.

Five years later, Sylvia suffered a nervous collapse,
burned the firehouse down. So sadistic had republican
Avondale become about the royalist Rosewaters that
Avondale laughed.

R

Sylvia was placed in a private mental hospital in
Indianapolis, was taken there by Eliot and Charley
Warmergran, the Fire Chief. They took her in the
Chief's car, which was a red Henry J with a siren on
top. They turned her over to a Dr. Ed Brown, a young
psychiatrist who later made his reputation describing her
illness. In the paper, he called Eliot and Sylvia *"Mr.
and Mrs. Z,"* and he called the town of Rosewater
"Hometown, U.S.A." He coined a new word for Sylvia's
disease, *"Samaritrophia,"* which he said meant,
*"hysterical indifference to the troubles of those less
fortunate than oneself."*

R

Norman Mushari now read Dr. Brown's treatise, which
was also in the confidential files of McAllister, Robjent,
Reed and McGee. His eyes were moist and soft and

brown, compelling him to see the pages as he saw the
world, as though through a quart of olive oil.

Samaritrophia, *he read,* is the suppression of an
overactive conscience by the rest of the mind.
"You must all take instructions from me!" the
conscience shrieks, in effect, to all the other
mental processes. The other processes try it for a
while, note that the conscience is unappeased,
that it continues to shriek, and they note, too,
that the outside world has not been even
microscopically improved by the unselfish acts
the conscience has demanded.

They rebel at last. They pitch the tyrannous
conscience down an oubliette, weld shut the
manhole cover of that dark dungeon. They can
hear the conscience no more. In the sweet silence,
the mental processes look about for a new leader,
and the leader most prompt to appear whenever
the conscience is stilled, Enlightened Self-interest,
does appear. Enlightened Self-interest gives them
a flag, which they adore on sight. It is essentially
the black and white Jolly Roger, with these words
written beneath the skull and crossbones, "The
hell with you, Jack, I've got mine!"

It seemed unwise to me, *Dr. Brown wrote and
Norman Mushari read slaveringly,* to set the noisy
conscience of Mrs. Z at liberty again. Neither
could I take much satisfaction in discharging her
while she was as heartless as Ilse Koch. I made it
the goal of my treatments, then, to keep her
conscience imprisoned, but to lift the lid of the
oubliette ever so slightly, so that the howls of the
prisoner might be very faintly heard. Through
trial and error with chemotherapy and electric
shock, this I achieved. I was not proud, for I had
calmed a deep woman by making her shallow. I

had blocked the underground rivers that
connected her to the Atlantic, Pacific, and Indian
Oceans, and made her content with being a
splash pool three feet across, four inches deep,
chlorinated, and painted blue.

Some doctor!

Some cure!

R

And some models the doctor was obliged to choose
in determining how much guilt and pity Mrs. Z
might safely be allowed to feel! The models were
persons with reputations for being normal. The
therapist, after a deeply upsetting investigation
of normality at this time and place, was bound
to conclude that a normal person, functioning
well on the upper levels of a prosperous,
industrialized society, can hardly hear his
conscience at all.

So a logical person might conclude that I have
been guilty of balderdash in announcing a new
disease samaritrophia, when it is virtually as
common among healthy Americans as noses, say.
I defend myself in this manner: samaritrophia is
only a disease, and a violent one, too, when it
attacks those exceedingly rare individuals who
reach biological maturity still loving and wanting
to help their fellow men.

I have treated only one case. I have never heard
of anyone's treating another. In looking about
myself, I can see only one other person who has
the potential for a samaritrophic collapse. That
person, of course, is Mr. Z. And so deep is his
commitment to compassion, that, were he to
come down with samaritrophia, I sense that he
would kill himself, or perhaps kill a hundred

others and then be shot down like a mad dog, before we could treat him.

R

Treat, treat, treat.

Some treat!

Mrs. Z, having been treated and cured in our health emporium, expressed a wish to, ". . . go out and have some fun for a change, to live it up . . ." before her looks were gone. Her looks were still staggeringly attractive, were marked by lines of affection unlimited, which she no longer deserved.

She wanted nothing more to do with Hometown or Mr. Z, announced that she was off to the gaiety of Paris, and to merry old friends there. She wished to buy new clothes, she said, and to dance and dance until she fainted in the arms of a tall, dark stranger, into the arms, hopefully, of a double spy.

She often referred to her husband as, "My dirty, drunk uncle down South," although never to his face. She was not a schizophrenic, but, whenever her husband visited her, which he did three times a week, she manifested all of the sick cutenesses of paranoia. Shades of Clara Bow! She would pluck his cheek, coax kisses from him, kisses she gigglingly declined to receive. She told him she wanted to go to Paris for just a little while, to see her dear family, and that she would be back before he knew it. She wanted him to say farewell and give her love to all her dear, underprivileged friends in Hometown.

Mr. Z was not deceived. He saw her off to Paris at the Indianapolis Airport, and he told me when the plane was a speck in the sky that he would never see her again. "She certainly looked happy," he said to me. "She certainly will have a good

time when she gets back there with the kind of
company she deserves."

He had used the word "certainly" twice. It
grated. And I knew intuitively that he was about
to grate me with it again. He did. "A lot of credit,"
he said, "certainly goes to you."

          R

I am informed by the woman's parents, who are
understandably ungrateful to Mr. Z, that he writes
and calls often. She does not open his letters.
She will not come to to the phone. And it is their
satisfied opinion that, as Mr. Z had hoped, she
is certainly happy.

     Prognosis: Another breakdown by-and-by.

          R

As for Mr. Z: He is certainly sick too, since he
certainly isn't like any other man I ever knew. He
will not leave Hometown, except for very short
trips as far as Indianapolis and no farther. I
suspect that he cannot leave Hometown. Why not?

     To be utterly unscientific, and science becomes
nauseating to a therapist after a case such as this:
His Destination is there.

     The good doctor's prognosis was correct. Sylvia
became a popular and influential member of the
international Jet Set, learned the many variations of the
Twist. She became known as the Duchess of Rosewater.
Many men proposed, but she was too happy to think of
either marriage or divorce. And then she fell to pieces
again in July of 1964.

     She was treated in Switzerland. She was discharged
six months later, silent and sad, almost unbearably
deep again. Eliot and the pitiful people of Rosewater

County again had a place in her consciousness. She wished to return to them, not out of yearning but out of a sense of duty. Her doctor warned her that a return might be fatal. He told her to remain in Europe, to divorce Eliot, and to build a quiet, meaningful life of her own.

So, very civilized divorce proceedings were begun, stage-managed by McAllister, Robjent, Reed and McGee.

R

Now it was time for Sylvia to fly to America for the divorce. And a meeting was held on a June evening in the Washington, D.C., apartment of Eliot's father, Senator Lister Ames Rosewater. Eliot was not there. He would not leave Rosewater County. Present were the Senator, Sylvia, Thurmond McAllister, the ancient lawyer, and his watchful young aide, Mushari.

R

The tone of the meeting was frank, sentimental, forgiving, sometimes hilarious, and fundamentally tragic always. There was brandy.

"In his heart," said the Senator, swirling his snifter, "Eliot doesn't love those awful people out there any more than I do. He couldn't possibly love them, if he weren't drunk all the time. I've said it before, and I'll say it again: This is basically a booze problem. If Eliot's booze were shut off, his compassion for the maggots in the slime on the bottom of the human garbage pail would vanish."

He clapped his hands, shook his old head. "If only there had been a child!" He was a product of St. Paul's and Harvard, but it pleased him to speak with the split-banjo twang of a Rosewater County hog farmer. He tore off his steel-rimmed spectacles, stared at his daughter-in-law with suffering blue eyes. "If only! If only!" He put his spectacles back on, spread his hands in resignation. The hands were as speckled as boxturtles. "The end of the Rosewater family is now plainly in view."

"There *are* other Rosewaters," McAllister suggested gently.

Mushari squirmed, for he meant to represent those others soon.

"I'm talking about *real* Rosewaters!" cried the Senator bitterly. "The *hell* with Pisquontuit!" Pisquontuit, Rhode Island, a seaside resort, was where the only other branch of the family lived.

"A buzzard feast, a buzzard feast," the Senator moaned, writhing in a masochistic fantasy of how the Rhode Island Rosewaters would pick the Indiana Rosewaters' bones. He coughed hackingly. The cough embarrassed him. He was a chain-smoker, like his son.

He went to the mantelpiece, glared at a colored photograph of Eliot there. The picture had been taken at the end of the Second World War. It showed a much-decorated captain of the Infantry. "So clean, so tall, so purposeful—so clean, so clean! He gnashed his crockery teeth. "What a noble mind is here o'erthrown!"

He scratched himself, though he did not itch. "How puffy and pasty he looks these days. I've seen healthier complexions on rhubarb pies! Sleeps in his underwear, eats a balanced diet of potato chips, Southern Comfort, and Rosewater Golden Lager Ambrosia Beer." He rattled his fingernails against the photograph. "Him! Him! Captain Eliot Rosewater—Silver Star, Bronze Star, Soldier's Medal, and Purple Heart with Cluster! Sailing champion! Ski champion! Him! Him! My God—the number of times life has said, 'Yes, yes, yes,' to him! Millions of dollars, hundreds of significant friends, the most beautiful, intelligent, talented, affectionate wife imaginable! A splendid education, an elegant mind in a big, clean, body—and what is his reply when life says nothing but, 'Yes, yes, yes'?

" 'No, no, no.'

"Why? Will someone tell me why?"

No one did.

R

"I had a female cousin one time—a Rockefeller, as it happened—" said the Senator, "and she confessed to me that she spent the fifteenth, sixteenth, and seventeenth years of her life saying nothing but, 'No, thank you.' Which is all very well for a girl of that age and station. But it would have been a damned unattractive trait in a *male* Rockefeller, and an even more unsuitable one, if I may say so, in a male Rosewater."

He shrugged. "Be that as it may, we *do* now have a male Rosewater who says 'No' to all the good things life would like to give him. He won't even live in the mansion any more." Eliot had moved out of the mansion and into an office when it became clear that Sylvia was never coming back to him.

"He could have been Governor of Indiana by lifting an eyebrow, could have been President of the United States, even, at the price of a few beads of sweat. And what is he? I ask you, what *is* he?"

The Senator coughed again, then answered his own question: "A notary public, friends and neighbors, whose commission is about to expire."

R

This was fairly true. The only official document that hung on the mildewed beaverboard wall of Eliot's busy office was his commission as a notary public. So many of the people who brought their troubles to him needed, among such a multitude of others things, someone to witness their signatures.

Eliot's office was on Main Street, a block northeast of the brick Parthenon, across the street from the new firehouse, which the Rosewater Foundation had built. It was a shotgun attic that spanned a lunchroom and a liquor store. There were only two windows, in doghouse dormers. Outside of one was a sign that said, *EATS.* Outside the other was a sign that said, *BEER.* Both signs were electrified and equipped with blinkers. And, as Eliot's father ranted in Washington about him, him, him, Eliot slept like a baby, and the signs blinked off and on.

Eliot made of his mouth a Cupid's bow, murmured something sweetly, turned over, snored. He was an athlete gone to lard, a big man, six-feet-three, two hundred thirty pounds, pale, balding on all sides of a wispy scalplock. He was swaddled in the elephant wrinkles of war-surplus long underwear. Written on gold letters on each of his windows, and on his street-level door, too, were these words:

*ROSEWATER FOUNDATION
HOW CAN WE HELP
YOU?*

5.

ELIOT SLEPT SWEETLY ON, although he had troubles
in droves.

It was the toilet in the foul little office lavatory that
seemed to be having all the bad dreams. It sighed, it
sobbed, it gurgled that it was drowning. Canned goods
and tax forms and *National Geographics* were piled on
the toilet tank. A bowl and a spoon were soaking in cold
water in the washbasin. The medicine cabinet over the
basin was wide open. It was crammed with vitamins and
headache remedies and hemorrhoid salves and laxatives
and sedatives. Eliot used them all regularly, but they
weren't for him alone. They were for all the vaguely ill
people who came to see him.

Love and understanding and a little money were not
enough for these people. They wanted medicine besides.

Papers were stacked everywhere—tax forms,
Veteran's Administration forms, pensions forms, relief
forms, Social Security forms, parole forms. Stacks had
toppled here and there, forming dunes. And between
the stacks and dunes lay paper cups and empty cans
of Ambrosia and cigarette butts and empty bottles of
Southern Comfort.

Thumbtacked to the walls were pictures Eliot had clipped from *Life* and *Look*, pictures that now rustled in a light cool breeze running before a thunderstorm. Eliot found that certain pictures cheered people up, particularly pictures of baby animals. His visitors also enjoyed pictures of spectacular accidents. Astronauts bored them. They liked pictures of Elizabeth Taylor because they hated her so much, felt very superior to her. Their favorite person was Abraham Lincoln. Eliot tried to popularize Thomas Jefferson and Socrates, too, but people couldn't remember from one visit to the next who they were. "Which one is which?" they'd say.

The office had once belonged to a dentist. There was no clue of this previous occupancy save for the staircase leading up from the street. The dentist had nailed tin signs to the risers, each sign praising some aspect of his services. The signs were still there, but Eliot had painted out the messages. He had written a new one, a poem by William Blake. This was it, as broken up so as to fit twelve risers:

> The Angel
> that presided
> o'er my
> birth said,
> "Little creature,
> form'd of
> Joy & Mirth,
> Go love
> without the
> help of
> any Thing
> on Earth."

At the foot of the stairs, written in pencil on the wall, by the Senator himself, was the Senator's rebuttal, another poem by Blake:

Love seeketh only Self to please,
To bind another to Its delight,
Joys in another's loss of ease,
And builds a Hell in Heaven's despite.

R

Back in Washington, Eliot's father was wishing out
loud that he and Eliot were both dead.

"I—I have a rather primitive idea," said McAllister.

"The last primitive idea you had cost me control of
eighty-seven million dollars."

McMAllister indicated with a tired smile that he wasn't
about to apologize for the design of the Foundation. It
had, after all, done exactly what it was meant to do,
had handed the fortune from father to son, without
the tax collector's getting a dime. McAllister could
scarcely have guaranteed that the son would be
conventional. "I should like to propose that Eliot and
Sylvia make one last try for a reconciliation."

Sylvia shook her head. "No," she whispered. "I'm
sorry. No." She was curled in a great wingchair. She
had taken off her shoes. Her face was a flawless
blue-white oval, her hair raven black. There were
circles under her eyes. "No."

This was, of course, a medical decision, and a wise
one, too. Her second breakdown and recovery had not
turned her back into the old Sylvia of the early
Rosewater County days. It had given her a distinctly new
personality, the third since her marriage to Eliot. The
core of this third personality was a feeling of
worthlessness, of shame at being revolted by the poor
and by Eliot's personal hygiene, and a suicidal wish to
ignore her revulsions, to get back to Rosewater, to very
soon die in a good cause.

So it was with self-conscious, medically-prescribed,
superficial opposition to total sacrfice that she said again,
"No."

R

The Senator swept Eliot's picture from the mantelpiece. "Who came blame her? One more roll in the hay with that drunk gypsy I call son?" He apologized for the coarseness of this last image. "Old men without hope have a tendency to be both crude and accurate. I beg your pardon."

Sylvia put her lovely head down, raised it again. "I don't think of him as that—as a drunk gypsy."

"I do, by God. Every time I'm forced to look at him I think to myself, 'What a staging area for a typhoid epidemic!' Don't try to spare my feelings, Sylvia. My son doesn't deserve a decent woman. He deserves what he's got, the sniveling camaraderie of whores, malingerers, pimps, and thieves."

"They're not that bad, Father Rosewater."

"As I understand it, that's their chief appeal to Eliot, that there's absolutely nothing good about them."

Sylvia, with two nervous breakdowns behind her, and with no well-formed dreams before her, said quietly, just as her doctor would have wanted her to, "I don't want to argue."

"You still *could* argue on Eliot's behalf?"

"Yes. If I don't make anything else clear tonight, at least let me make that clear: Eliot is right to do what he's doing. It's beautiful what he's doing. I'm simply not strong enough or good enough to be by his side any more. The fault is mine."

Pained mystification, and then helplessness, suffused the Senator's face. "Tell me one good thing about those people Eliot helps."

"I can't."

"I thought not."

"It's a secret thing," she said, forced to argue, pleading for the argument to stop right there.

Without any notion of how merciless he was being, the Senator pressed on. "You're among friends now—

suppose you tell us what this great secret is."

"The secret is that they're human," said Sylvia. She looked from face to face for some flicker of understanding. There was none. The last face into which she peered was Norman Mushari's. Mushari gave her a hideously inappropriate smile of greed and fornication.

Sylvia excused herself abruptly, went into the bathroom and wept.

R

Thunder was heard in Rosewater now, caused a brindle dog to come scrambling out of the firehouse with psychosomatic rabies. The dog stopped in the middle of the street, shivering. The street lights were faint and far apart. The only other illumination came from a blue bulb in front of the police station in the courthouse basement, a red bulb in front of the firehouse, and a white bulb in the telephone booth across the street from the Saw City Kandy Kitchen, which was the bus depot, too.

There was a *crash*. Lightning turned everything to blue-white diamonds.

The dog ran to the door of the Rosewater Foundation, scratched and howled. Upstairs, Eliot slept on. His sickly translucent drip-dry shirt, which hung from a ceiling fixture, swayed like a ghost.

R

Eliot had only one shirt. He had only one suit—a frowzy, blue, double-breasted chalkstripe now hanging on the knob of the lavatory door. It was a wonderfully made suit, for it still held together, though it was very old. Eliot had gotten it in trade from a volunteer fireman in New Egypt, New Jersey, way back in 1952.

Eliot had only one pair of shoes, black ones. They had a crackle finish as a result of an experiment. Eliot

once tried to polish them with Johnson's *Glo-Coat,*
which was a floorwax, not intended for shoes. One shoe
was on his desk. The other was in the lavatory, on the
rim of the washbasin. A maroon nylon sock, with garter
attached, was in each shoe. One end of the garter of
the sock in the shoe on the washbasin was in the water.
It had saturated itself and its sock, too, through the magic
of capillary action.

The only colorful, new articles in the office, other than
the magazine pictures, were a family-size box of *Tide,*
the washday miracle, and the yellow slicker and red
helmet of a volunteer fireman, which hung on pegs by
the office door. Eliot was a Fire Lieutenant. He could
easily have been Captain or Chief, since he was a
devoted and skilful fireman, and had given the Fire
Department six new engines besides. It was at his own
insistence that he held a rank no higher than Lieutenant.

Eliot, because he almost never left his office except
to fight fires, was the man to whom all fire calls were
sent. That was why he had two telephones by his cot.
The black one was for Foundation calls. The red one
was for fire calls. When a fire call came in, Eliot would
push a red button mounted on the wall under his
commission as a Notary Public. The button activated
a doomsday bullhorn under the cupola on top of the
firehouse. Eliot had paid for the horn, and the cupola,
too.

There was an earsplitting thunderclap.

"Now, now—now, now," said Eliot in his sleep.

His black telephone was about to ring. Eliot would
awake and answer it by the third ring. He would say
what he said to every caller, no matter what the hour:

"This is the Rosewater Foundation. How can we help
you?"

R

It was the Senator's conceit that Eliot trafficked with

criminals. He was mistaken. Most of Eliot's clients
weren't brave enough or clever enough for lives of crime.
But Eliot, particularly when he argued with his father
or bankers or his lawyers, was almost equally mistaken
about who his clients were. He would argue that the
people he was trying to help were the same sorts of
people who, in generations past, had cleared the forests,
drained the swamps, built the bridges, people whose
sons formed the backbone of the infantry in time of
war—and so on. The people who leaned on Eliot
regularly were a lot weaker than that—and dumber,
too. When it came time for their sons to go into the
Armed Forces, for instance, the sons were generally
rejected as being mentally, morally, and physically
undesirable.

There was a tough element among the Rosewater
County poor who, as a matter of pride, stayed away
from Eliot and his uncritical love, who had the guts
to get out of Rosewater County and look for work in
Indianapolis or Chicago or Detroit. Very few of them
found steady work in those places, of course, but at
least they tried.

R

The client who was about to make Eliot's black
telephone ring was a sixty-eight-year-old virgin who,
by almost anybody's standards, was too dumb to live.
Her name was Diana Moon Glampers. No one had ever
loved her. There was no reason why anyone should.
She was ugly, stupid, and boring. On the rare occasions
when she had to introduce herself, she always said her
full name, and followed that with the mystifying
equation that had thrust her into life so pointlessly:

"My mother was a Moon. My father was a Glampers."

R

This cross between a Glampers and a Moon was a
domestic servant in the tapestry-brick Rosewater
Mansion, the legal residence of the Senator, a house he
actually occupied no more than ten days out of any
year. During the remaining 355 days of each year,
Diana had the twenty-six rooms all to herself. She
cleaned and cleaned and cleaned alone, without even
the luxury of having someone to blame for making dirt.

When Diana was through for the day, she would
retire to a room over the Rosewater's six-car garage.
The only vehicles in the garage were a 1936 Ford
Phaeton, which was up on blocks, and a red tricycle
with a fire bell hanging from the handlebars. The
tricycle had belonged to Eliot as a child.

After work Diana would sit in her room and listen
to her cracked green plastic radio, or she would fumble
with her Bible. She could not read. Her Bible was a
frazzled wreck. On the table beside her bed was a white
telephone, a so-called Princess telephone, which she
rented from the Indiana Bell Telephone Company for
seventy-five cents a month, over and above ordinary
service charges.

There was a thunderclap.

Diana yelled for help. She should have yelled.
Lightning had killed her mother and father at a
Rosewater Lumber Company picnic in 1916. She was
sure lightning was going to kill her, too. And, because
her kidneys hurt all the time, she was sure the lightning
would hit her in the kidneys.

She snatched her Princess phone from its cradle.
She dialed the only number she ever dialed. She
whimpered and moaned, waiting for the person at the
other end to answer.

It was Eliot. His voice was sweet, vastly paternal—as
humane as the lowest note of a cello. "This is the

Rosewater Foundation," he said. "How can we help
you?"

R

"The electricity is after me again, Mr. Rosewater. I
had to call! I'm so *scared!*"

"Call any time you want, dear. That's what I'm here
for."

"The electricity is *really* gonna get me this time."

"Oh, darn that electricity." Eliot's anger was
sincere. "That electricity makes me so mad, the way it
torments you all the time. It isn't fair."

"I wish it would come ahead and kill me, instead of
just talk about it all the time."

"This would be a mighty sad town, dear, if that ever
happened."

"Who'd care?"

"I'd care."

"You care about everybody. I mean who else?"

"Many, many, many people, dear."

"Dumb old woman—sixty-eight years old."

"Sixty-eight is a wonderful age."

"Sixty-eight years is a long time for a body to live
without having one nice thing ever happen to the body.
Nothing nice ever happened to me. How could it? I was
behind the door when the good Lord passed out the
brains."

"That is not *true!*"

"I was behind the door when the good Lord passed
out the strong, beautiful bodies. Even when I was young,
I couldn't run fast, couldn't jump. I have never felt real
good—not once. I have had gas and swole ankles and
kiddley pains since I was a baby. And I was behind the
door when the good Lord passed out the money and
the good luck, too. And when I got nerve enough to
come out from behind the door and whisper, 'Lord,

Lord—dear, sweet Lord—here's little old me'—wasn't
one nice thing left. He had to give me an old potato for
a nose. He had to give me hair like steel wool, and had
to give me a voice like a bullfrog."

"It isn't a bullfrog voice at all, Diana. It's a lovely
voice."

"Bullfrog voice," she insisted. "There was this bullfrog
up there in Heaven, Mr. Rosewater. The good Lord
was going to send it down to this sad world to be born,
but that old bullfrog was smart. 'Sweet Lord,' that smart
old bullfrog said, 'if it's all the same to you, Sweet
Lord, I'd just as soon not be born. It don't look like
much fun for a *frog* down there.' So the Lord let that
bullfrog hop around in Heaven up there, where nobody'd
use it for bait or eat its legs, and the Lord gave *me*
that bullfrog's voice."

R

There was another thunderclap. It raised Diana's voice
an octave. "I should have said what that bullfrog said!
This ain't such a hot world for Diana Moon Glamperses,
neither!"

R

"Now, now, Diana—now, now," said Eliot. He took a
small drink from a bottle of Southern Comfort.

"My kiddleys hurt me all day, Mr. Rosewater. They
feel like a red-hot cannonball of electricity was going
through them real slow, and just turning round and
round, with poisoned razorblades sticking out of it."

"That can't be very pleasant."

"It ain't."

"I *do* wish you'd go see a doctor about those darn
kidneys, dear."

"I did. I went to Dr. Winters today, just like you told

me. He treated me like I was a cow and he was a drunk veterinarian. And when he was through punching me and rolling me all around, why he just laughed. He said he wished everybody in Rosewater County had kiddleys as wonderful as mine. He said my kiddley trouble was all in my head. Oh, Mr. Rosewater, from now on you're the only doctor for me."

"I'm not a doctor, dear."

"I don't care. You've cured more hopeless diseases than all the doctors in Indiana put together."

"Now, now—"

"Dawn Leonard had boils for ten years, and you cured 'em. Ned Calvin had that twitch in his eye since he was a little boy, and you made it stop. Pearl Flemming came and saw you, and she threw her crutch away. And now my kiddleys have stopped hurting, just hearing your sweet voice."

"I'm glad."

"And the thunder and lightning's stopped."

It was true. There was only the hopelessly sentimental music of rainfall now.

R

"So you can sleep now, dear?"

"Thanks to you. Oh, Mr. Rosewater, there should be a big statue of you in the middle of this town—made out of diamonds and gold, and precious rubies' beyond price, and pure uranimum. You, with your great name and your fine education and your money and the nice manners your mother taught you—you could have been off in some big city, riding around in Cadillacs with the highest muckety-mucks, while the bands played and the crowds cheered. You could have been so high and mighty in this world, that when you looked down on the plain, dumb, ordinary people of poor old Rosewater County, we would look like bugs."

"Now, now—"

"You gave up everything a man is supposed to want, just to help the little people, and the little people know it. God bless you, Mr. Rosewater. Good night."

6.

"NATURE'S LITTLE DANGER SIGNALS—" Senator
Rosewater said to Sylvia and McAllister and Mushari
darkly. "How many did I miss? All of them, I guess."

"Don't blame yourself," said McAllister.

"If a man has but one child," said the Senator, "and
the family is famous for producing unusual, strong-willed
individuals, what standards can the man have for
deciding whether or not his child is a nut?"

"Don't *blame* yourself!"

"I have spent my life demanding that people blame
themselves for their misfortunes."

"You've made exceptions."

"Damn few."

"Include yourself among the damn few. That's where
you belong."

"I often think that Eliot would not have turned out
as he has, if there hadn't been all that whoop-dee-doo
about his being mascot of the Fire Department when
he was a child. God, how they spoiled him—let him
ride on the seat of the Number One Pumper, let him
ring the bell—taught him how to make the truck backfire
by turning the ignition off and on, laughed like crazy
when he blew the muffler off. They all smelled of
booze, of course, too—" He nodded and blinked.
"Booze and fire engines—a happy childhood regained.

I don't know, I don't know, I just don't know.
Whenever we went out there, I told him it was home—
but I never thought he would be dumb enough to
believe it."

R

"I blame myself," said the Senator.

"Good for you," said McAllister. "And, while you're
at it, be sure to hold yourself responsible for everything
that happened to Eliot during World War Two. It's
your fault, without a doubt, that all those firemen were
in that smoke-filled building."

McAllister was speaking of the proximate cause of
Eliot's nervous breakdown near the end of the war. The
smoke-filled building was a clarinet factory in Bavaria.
It was supposedly infested by a hedgehog of S.S. troops.

Eliot led a platoon from his company in an assault
on the building. His customary weapon was a Thompson
submachinegun. But he went in with a rifle and fixed
bayonet this time, because of the danger of shooting one
of his own men in the smoke. He had never stuck a
bayonet into anybody before, not in years of carnage.

He pitched a grenade into a window. When it went
off, Captain Rosewater went through the window
himself, found himself standing in a sea of very still
smoke whose undulating surface was level with his eyes.
He tilted his head back to keep his nose in air. He
could hear Germans, but he couldn't see them.

He took a step forward, stumbled over one body, fell
on another. They were Germans who had been killed
by his grenade. He stood up, found himself face-to-face
with a helmeted German in a gas mask.

Eliot, like the good soldier he was, jammed his knee
into the man's groin, drove his bayonet into his throat,
withdrew the bayonet, smashed the man's jaw with his
rifle butt.

And then Eliot heard an American sergeant yelling somewhere off to his left. This visibility was apparently a lot better over there, for the sergeant was yelling, "Cease fire! Hold your fire, you guys. Jesus Christ—these aren't soldiers. They're firemen!"

It was true: Eliot had killed three unarmed firemen. They were ordinary villagers, engaged in the brave and and uncontroversial business of trying to keep a building from combining with oxygen.

When the medics got the masks off the three Eliot had killed, they proved to be two old men and a boy. The boy was the one Eliot had bayoneted. He didn't look more than fourteen.

Eliot seemed reasonably well for about ten minutes after that. And then he calmly lay down in front of a moving truck.

The truck stopped in time, but the wheels were touching Captain Rosewater. When some of his horrified men picked him up, they found out Eliot was stiff, so rigid that they might have carried him by his hair and his heels.

He stayed like that for twelve hours, and would not speak or eat—so they shipped him back to Gay Paree.

R

"What did he seem like there in Paris?" the Senator wanted to know. "Did he seem sane enough to you then?"

"That's how I happened to meet him."

"I don't understand."

"Father's string quartet played for some of the mental patients in one of the American hospitals—and Father got talking to Eliot, and Father thought Eliot was the sanest American he had ever met. When Eliot was well enough to leave, Father had him to dinner. I remember Father's introduction: 'I want you all to meet the only

American who has so far noticed the Second World War.' "

"What did he say that was so *sane?*"

"It was the impression he made, really—more than— than the particular things he said. I remember how my father described him. He said, 'This young Captain I'm bringing home—he despises art. Can you imagine? *Despises* it—and yet he does it in such a way that I can't help loving him for it. What he's saying I think, is that art has failed him, which I must admit, is a very fair thing for a man who has bayoneted a fourteen-year-old boy in the line of duty to say.' "

"I loved Eliot on sight."

"Isn't there some other word you could use?"

"Than what?"

"Than *love.*"

"What better word *is* there?"

"It was a perfectly good word—until Eliot got hold of it. It's spoiled for me now. Eliot did to the word *love* what the Russians did to the word *democracy.* If Eliot is going to love everybody, no matter what they are, no matter what they do, then those of us who love particular people for particular reasons had better find ourselves a new word." He looked up at an oil painting of his deceased wife. "For instance—I loved *her* more than I loved our garbage collector, which makes me guilty of the most unspeakable of modern crimes: *Dis-crim-i-nay-tion.*"

R

Sylvia smiled wanly. "For want of a better word, could I go on using the old one—just for tonight?"

"On your lips it still has meaning."

"I loved him on sight in Paris—and I love him when I think of him now."

"You must have realized pretty early in the game that you had a nut on your hands."

"There was the drinking."

"There's the heart of the problem right there!"

"And there was that awful business with Arthur Garvey Ulm." Ulm was a poet Eliot had given ten thousand dollars to when the Foundation was still in New York.

"That poor Arthur told Eliot he wanted to be free to tell the truth, regardless of the economic consequences, and Eliot wrote him a tremendous check right then and there. It was at a cocktail party," said Sylvia. "I remember Arthur Godfrey was there—and Robert Frost—and Salvador Dali—and a lot of others, too.

" 'You go tell the truth, by God. It's about time somebody did,' Eliot said to him. 'And if you need any more money to tell more truth, you just come back to me.'

"Poor Arthur wandered around the party in a daze, showing people the check, asking them if it could possibly be real. They all told him it was a perfectly wonderful check, and he came back to Eliot, made sure again that the check was not a joke. And then, almost hysterically, he begged Eliot to tell him what he should write about.

" 'The truth!' said Eliot.

" 'You're my patron—and I thought that as my patron you—you might—'

" 'I'm not your patron. I'm a fellow-American who's paying your money to find out what the truth is. That's a very different sort of thing.'

" 'Right, right,' said Arthur. 'That's the way it should be. That's the way I want it. I just thought there was maybe some special subject you—'

" '*You* pick the subject, and be good and fearless about it.'

" 'Right.' And before he knew what he was doing, poor Arthur saluted, and I don't think he'd even been in the Army or Navy or anything. And he left Eliot, but he went around the party again, asking everybody what sorts of things Eliot was interested in. He finally came back to tell Eliot that he had once been a migratory fruit-picker, and that he wanted to write a cycle of poems about how miserable the fruit pickers were.

"Eliot drew himself up to his full height, looked down on Arthur, his eyes blazing, and he said, so that everybody could hear, 'Sir! Do you realize that the Rosewaters are the founders and the majority stockholders in the United Fruit Company?' "

"That wasn't true!" said the Senator.

"Of course it wasn't," said Sylvia.

"Did the Foundation have any United Fruit stock at all at that time?" the Senator asked McAllister.

"Oh—five thousand shares, maybe."

"Nothing."

"Nothing," McAllister agreed.

"Poor Arthur turned crimson, slunk away, came back again, asked Eliot very humbly who his favorite poet was. ' I don't know his name,' said Eliot, 'and I wish I did, because it's the only poem I ever thought enough of to commit to heart.'

" 'Where did you see it?'

" 'It was written on a wall, Mr. Ulm, of the men's room of a beer joint on the border between Rosewater and Brown Counties in Indiana, the Log Cabin Inn.' "

"Oh, this is weird, this is weird," said the Senator. "The Log Cabin Inn must have burned down—oh God —in 1934 or so. How weird that Eliot should remember it."

"Was he ever in it?" McAllister asked.

"Once—just once, now that I think back," said the Senator. "It was a dreadful robbers' roost, and we would never have stopped there if the car hadn't boiled over. Eliot must have been—ten?—twelve? And he probably *did* use the men's room, and he probably did see something written on the wall, something he never forgot." He nodded. "How weird, how weird."

"What was the poem?" said McAllister.

Sylvia apologized to the two old men for having to be coarse, and then she recited the two lines Eliot had recited loudly for Ulm:

> "We don't piss in your ashtrays,
>> So please don't throw cigarettes in our urinals."

R

"The poor poet fled in tears," said Sylvia. "For months after that I was in terror of opening small packages, lest one of them contain the ear of Arthur Garvey Ulm."

R

"Hates the arts," said McAllister. He clucked.

"He's a poet himself," said Sylvia.

"That's news to me," said the Senator. "I never saw any of it."

"He used to write me poems sometimes."

"He's probably happiest when writing on the walls of public lavatories. I often wondered who did it. Now I know. It's my poetic son."

"*Does* he write on lavatory walls?" McAllister asked.

"I heard that he did," said Sylvia. "It was innocent— it wasn't obscene. During the New York days, people told me Eliot was writing the same message in men's rooms all over town."

"Do you remember what it was?"

"Yes. '*If you would be unloved and forgotten, be reasonable.*' As far I know, that was original with him."

R

At that moment Eliot was trying to read himself back

to sleep with the manuscript of a novel by none other than Arthur Garvey Ulm.

The name of the book was *Get With Child a Mandrake Root,* a line from a poem by John Donne. The dedication read, "For Eliot Rosewater, my compassionate turquoise." And under that was another quotation from Donne:

> A compassionate turquoise which doth tell
> By looking pale, the wearer is not well.

A covering letter from Ulm explained that the book was going to be published by Palindrome Press in time for Christmas, and was going to be a joint selection, along with *The Cradle of Erotica,* of a major book club.

> You have no doubt forgotten me, Compassionate Turquoise, *the letter said in part.* The Arthur Garvey Ulm you knew was a man well worth forgetting. What a coward he was, and what a fool he was to think he was a poet! And what a long, long time it took him to understand exactly how generous and kind your cruelty was! How much you managed to tell me about what was wrong with me, and what I should do about it, and how few words you used! Here then (fourteen years later) are eight hundred pages of prose by me. They could not have been created by me without you, and I do not mean your money. (Money is shit, which is one of things I have tried to say in the book.) I mean your insistence that the truth be told about this sick, sick society of ours, and that the words for the telling could be found on the walls of restrooms.

Eliot couldn't remember who Arthur Garvey Ulm was, and so was even further from knowing what advice he might have given the man. The clues Ulm offered were so nebulous. Eliot was pleased that he had given someone useful advice, was thrilled even, when Ulm declared:

> "Let them shoot me, let them hang me, but I have told the truth. The gnashing of the teeth of the Pharisees, Madison Avenue phonies and Philistines will be music to my ears. With your divine assistance, I have let the Djin of truth about them out of the bottle, and they will never, never, never ever get it back in!"

Eliot began to read avidly the truths Ulm expected to get killed for telling:

> "CHAPTER ONE
> "I twisted her arm until she opened her legs, and she gave a little scream, half joy, half pain (how do you figure a woman?), as I rammed the old avenger home."

Eliot found him possessed of an erection. "Oh, for heaven's sakes," he said to his procreative organ, "how irrelevant can you be?"

R

"If only there had been a child," said the Senator again. And then the density of his regret was penetrated by this thought: That it was cruel of him to speak so to the woman who had failed to bear the magic child. "Excuse an old fool, Sylvia. I can understand why you might thank God there is no child."

Sylvia, returned from her cry in the bathroom, experimented with small gestures, all indicating that she would have loved such a baby, but that she might have pitied it, too. "I would never thank God for a thing like *that*."

"May I ask you a highly personal question?"

"It's what life does all the time."

"Do you think it is remotely possible that he will *ever* reproduce?"

"I haven't seen him for three years."

"I'm asking you to make an extrapolation."

"I can only tell you," she said, "that, toward the end of our marriage, love-making was something less than a mania with us both. He was once a sweet fanatic for love-making, but not for making children of his own."

The Senator clucked ruefully. "If only I had taken proper care of *my* child!" He winced. "I paid a call to the psychoanalyst Eliot used to go to in New York. Finally got around to it last year. I seem to get around to everything about Eliot twenty years too late. The thing is—the thing is—I—I've never been able to get it through my head that such a splendid animal could ever go so much to hell!"

Mushari concealed his hunger for clinical details of Eliot's ailment, waited tensely for someone to urge the Senator to continue. No one did so, Mushari exposed himself. "And what did the doctor say?"

The Senator, suspecting nothing, resumed his tale: "These people never want to talk about what *you* want to talk about. It's always something else. When he found out who I was, he didn't want to talk about Eliot. He wanted to talk about the Rosewater Law." The Rosewater Law was what the Senator thought of as his legislative masterpiece. It made the publication or possession of obscene materials a Federal offense, carrying penalties up to fifty thousand dollars and ten years in prison, without hope of parole. It was a masterpiece because it actually defined obscenity.

> Obscenity, *it said,* is any picture or phonograph record or any written matter calling attention to reproductive organs, bodily discharges, or bodily hair.

"This psychoanalyst," the Senator complained,

"wanted to know about *my* childhood. He wanted to go
into my feelings about bodily hair." The Senator
shuddered. "I asked him to kindly get off the subject,
that my revulsions were shared, so far as I knew, by
all decent men." He pointed to McAllister, simply
wanting to point at someone, anyone. "There's your
key to pornography. Other people say, 'Oh, how can you
recognize it, how can you tell it from art and all that?'
I've written the key into law! The difference between
pornography and art is bodily hair!"

He flushed, apologized abjectly to Sylvia. "I beg
your pardon, my dear."

Mushari had to prod him again. "And the doctor
didn't say *anything* about Eliot?"

"The damn doctor said Eliot never told him a damn
thing but well-known facts from history, almost all of
them related to the oppression of odd-balls or the poor.
He said any diagnosis he made of Eliot's disease would
have to be irresponsible speculation. As a deeply
worried father, I told the doctor, 'Go ahead and guess
as much as you want to about my son. I won't hold you
responsible. I'd be most grateful if you'd say anything,
true or not, because I ran out of ideas about my boy,
responsible or irresponsible, true or not, years ago.
Stick your stainless steel spoon in this unhappy old
man's brains, Doctor,' I told him, 'and stir.'

"He said to me, 'Before I tell you what my
irresponsible thoughts are, I'll have to discuss sexual
perversion some. I intend to involve Eliot in the
discussion—so, if an involvement of that sort would
affect you violently, let's have our talk come to an end
right here.' 'Carry on,' I said. 'I'm an old futz, and the
theory is that an old futz can't be hurt very much by
anything anybody says. I've never believed it before, but
I'll try to believe it now.'

"'Very well—' he said, let's assume that a healthy
young man is supposed to be sexually aroused by an

attractive woman not his mother or sister. If he's aroused by other things, another man, say, or an umbrella or the ostrich boa of the Empress Josephine or a sheep or a corpse or his mother or a stolen garterbelt, he is what we call a *pervert*.'

"I replied that I had always known such people were about, but that I'd never thought much about them because there didn't seem to be much *to* think about them.

" 'Good,' he said. 'That's a calm, reasonable reaction, Senator Rosewater, that I'm frank to say surprises me. Let us hasten on to the admission that every case of perversion is essentially a case of crossed wires. Mother Nature and Society order a man to take his sex to such and such a place and do thus and so with it. Because of the crossed wires, the unhappy man enthusiastically goes straight to the wrong place, proudly, vigorously does some hideously inappropriate thing; and he can count himself lucky if he is simply crippled for life by a police force rather than killed by a mob.'

"I began to feel terror for the first time in many years," said the Senator, "and I told the doctor so.

" 'Good,' he said again. 'The most exquisite pleasure in the practice of medicine comes from nudging a layman in the direction of terror, then bringing him back to safety again. Eliot certainly has his wires crossed, but the inappropriate thing to which the short circuit has caused him to bring his sexual energies isn't necessarily such a very bad thing.'

" 'What *is* it?' I cried, thinking in spite of myself of Eliot stealing women's underwear, of Eliot snipping off locks of hair on subways, of Eliot as a Peeping Tom." The Senator from Indiana shuddered. " 'Tell me, Doctor—tell me the worst. Eliot is bringing his sexual energies to what?'

" 'To Utopia,' he said."

Frustration made Norman Mushari sneeze.

7.

ELIOT'S EYELIDS were growing heavy as he read
Get With Child a Mandrake Root. He was rumpling
about in it at random, hoping to find by chance the
words that were supposed to make Pharisees gnash their
teeth. He found one place where a judge was damned
for never having given his wife an orgasm, and another
where an advertising executive in charge of a soap
account got drunk, locked his apartment doors, and put
on his mother's wedding dress. Eliot frowned, tried to
think that that sort of thing was fair-to-middling
Pharisee-baiting, failed to think so.

He read now the account executive's fiancée's
seduction of her father's chauffeur. Suggestively, she bit
off the breast-pocket buttons of his uniform jacket. Eliot
Rosewater fell fast asleep.

The telephone rang three times.

"This is the Rosewater Foundation. How can we help
you?"

"Mr. Rosewater—" said a fretful man, "you don't
know me."

"Did someone tell you that mattered?"

"I'm nothing, Mr. Rosewater. I'm worse than nothing."

"Then God made a pretty bad mistake, didn't he?"

"He sure did when he made me."

"Maybe you brought your complaint to the right place."

"What kind of a place *is* it, anyway?"

"How did you happen to hear of us?"

"There's this big black and yellow sticker in the phone booth. Says, *'Don't Kill Yourself. Call the Rosewater Foundation,'* and it's got your number." Such stickers were in every phone booth in the county, and in the back windows of the cars and trucks of most of the volunteer firemen, too. "You know what somebody's written right under that in pencil?"

"No."

"Says, *'Eliot Rosewater is a saint. He'll give you love and money. If you'd rather have the best piece of tail in southern Indiana, call Melissa.'* And then it's got *her* number."

"You're a stranger in these parts?"

"I'm a stranger in all parts. But what *are* you anyway —some kind of religion?"

"Two-Seed-in-the-Spirit Predestinarian Baptist."

"What?"

"That's what I generally say when people insist I must have a religion. There happens to *be* such a sect, and I'm sure it's a good one. Foot-washing is practiced, and the ministers draw no pay. I wash my feet, and I draw no pay."

"I don't get it," said the caller.

"Just a way of trying to put you at ease, to let you know you don't have to be deadly serious with me. You don't happen to *be* a Two-Seed-in-the-Spirit Predestinarian Baptist, do you?"

"Jesus, no."

"There are two hundred people who *are,* and sooner or later I'm going to say to one of them what I've just said to you." Eliot took a drink. "I live in dread of that moment—and it's sure to come."

"You sound like a drunk. It sounded like you just took a drink."

"Be that as it may—what can we do to help you?"

"Who the hell *are* you?"

"The Government."

"The what?"

"The Government. If I'm not a Church, and I still want to keep people from killing themselves, I must be the Government. Right?"

The man muttered something.

"Or the Community Chest," said Eliot.

"Is this some kind of joke?"

"That's for me to know and you to find out."

"Maybe you think it's funny to put up signs about people who want to commit suicide."

"Are *you* about to?"

"And what if I was?"

"I wouldn't tell you the gorgeous reasons *I* have discovered for going on living."

"What *would* you do?"

"I'd ask you to name the rock-bottom price you'd charge to go on living for just one more week."

There was a silence.

"Did you hear me?" said Eliot.

"I heard you."

"If you're not going to kill yourself, would you please hang up? There are other people who'd like to use the line."

"You sound so crazy."

"You're the one who wants to kill himself."

"What if I said I wouldn't live through the next week for a million dollars?"

"I'd say, 'Go ahead and die.' Try a thousand."

"A thousand."

"Go ahead and die. Try a hundred."

"A hundred."

"Now you're making sense. Come on over and talk." He told him where his office was. "Don't be afraid of

the dogs in front of the firehouse," he said. "They only
bite when the fire horn goes off."

R

About the fire horn: To the best of Eliot's knowledge,
it was the loudest alarm in the Western Hemisphere. It
was driven by a seven-hundred-horsepower
Messerschmitt engine that had a thirty-horsepower
electric starter. It had been the main air-raid siren of
Berlin during the Second World War. The Rosewater
Foundation had bought it from the West German
government and presented it to the town anonymously.

When it arrived by flatcar, the only clue as to the
donor was a small tag that said, simply: "Compliments
of a friend."

R

Eliot wrote in a cumbersome ledger he kept under his
cot. It was bound in pebbled black leather, had three
hundred ruled pages of eye-rest green. He called it his
Domesday Book. It was in this book, from the very
first day of the Foundation's operations in Rosewater,
that Eliot entered the name of each client, the nature
of the client's pains, and what the Foundation had done
about them.

The book was nearly full, and only Eliot or his
estranged wife could have interpreted all that was
written there. What he wrote now was the name of
the suicidal man who had called him, who had come to
see him, who had just departed—departed a little
sulkily, as though suspecting that he had been swindled
or mocked, but couldn't imagine how or why.

"Sherman Wesley Little," wrote Eliot. *"Indy,
Su-TDM-LO-V2-W3K3-K2CP-RF $300."* Decoded,
this meant that Little was from Indianapolis, was a
suicidal tool-and-die maker who had been laid off, a

veteran of the Second World War with a wife and three
children, the second child suffering from cerebral palsy.
Eliot had awarded him a Rosewater Fellowship of $300.

A prescription that was far more common than
money in the Domesday Book was "AW." This
represented Eliot's recommendation to people who were
down in the dumps for every reason and for no reason
in particular: "Dear, I tell you what to do—take an
aspirin tablet, and wash it down with a glass of wine."

R

"FH" stood for "Fly Hunt." People often felt a
desperate need to do something nice for Eliot. He
would ask them to come at a specific time in order to
rid his office of flies. During the fly season, this was an
Augean task, for Eliot had no screens on his windows,
and his office, moreover, was connected directly to the
foul kitchen of the lunchroom below by means of a
greasy hot-air register in the floor.

So the fly hunts were actually rituals, and were
ritualized to such an extent that conventional fly-swatters
were not used, and men and women hunted flies in very
different ways. The men used rubber bands, and the
women used tumblers of lukewarm water and soapsuds.

The rubber-band technique worked like this: A man
would slice through a rubber band, making it a strand
rather than a loop. He would stretch the strand between
his hands, sight down the strand as though it were a
rifle barrel, let it snap when a fly was in his sights. A
well-hit fly would often be vaporized, accounting for
the peculiar color of Eliot's walls and woodwork, which
was largely dried fly purée.

The tumbler-and-soapsuds technique worked like this:
A woman would look for a fly hanging upside down.
She would then bring her tumbler of suds directly
under the fly very slowly, taking advantage of the fact

that an upside-down fly, when approached by danger, will drop straight down two inches or more, in a free fall, before using his wings. Ideally, the fly would not sense danger until it was directly below him, and he would obligingly drop into the suds to be caught, to work his way down through the bubbles, to drown.

Of this technique Eliot often said: "Nobody believes it until she tries it. Once she finds out it works, she never wants to quit."

R

In the back of the ledger was a very unfinished novel which Eliot had begun years before, on an evening when he understood at last that Sylvia would never come back to him.

Why do so many souls voluntarily return to Earth after failing and dying, failing and dying, failing and dying there? Because Heaven is such a null. Over Dem Pearly Gates these words should be embalzoned:

A LITTLE NOTHING, O GOD, GOES A LONG, LONG WAY.

But the only written on the infinite portal of Paradise are the grafitti of vandal souls. "Welcome to the Bulgarian World's Fair!" says a penciled plaint on a pediment of pearl. "Better red than dead," another opines.

"You ain't a man till you've had black meat," suggests another. And this has been revised to read, "You ain't a man till you've *been* black meat."

"Where can I get a good lay around here?" asks a bawdy soul, drawing this reply: "Try 'Lay of the Last Minstrel,' by Alfred, Lord Tennyson."
My own contribution:

Those who write on Heaven's walls

Should mold their shit in little balls.
And those who read these lines of wit
Should eat these little balls of shit.

        R

"Kublai Khan, Napoleon, Julius Caesar and King
Richard the Lion Hearted all stink," a brave soul
declares. The claim is unchallenged, nor are
challenges from the parties insulted likely. The
immortal soul of Kublai Khan now inhabits the
meek meat of a veterinarian's wife in Lima, Peru.
The immortal soul of Bonaparte peers out from
the hot and stuffy meat of the fourteen-year-old
son of the Harbor Master of Cotuit, Massachusetts.
Great Caesar's ghost manages as best it can with
the syphilitic meat of a Pygmy widow in the
Andaman Islands. Coeur de Lion has found himself
once again taken captive during his travels,
imprisoned this time in the flesh of Coach
Letzinger, a pitiful exhibitionist and freelance
garbage man in Rosewater, Indiana. Coach, with
poor old King Richard inside, goes to Indianapolis
on the Greyhound bus three or four times a year,
dresses up for the trip in shoes, socks, garters, a
raincoat, and a chromium-plated whistle hung
around his neck. When he gets to Indianapolis,
Coach goes to the silver department of one of
the big stores, where there are always a lot of
brides-to-be picking out silver patterns. Coach
blows his whistle, all the girls look, Coach throws
open his raincoat, closes it again, and runs like
hell to catch the bus back to Rosewater.

        R

Heaven is the bore of bores, *Eliot's novel went on,*
so most wraiths queue up to be reborn—and they

live and love and fail and die, and they queue up
to be reborn again. They take pot luck, as the
saying goes. They don't gibber and squeak to be
one race or another, one sex or another, one
nationality or another, one class or another.
What they want and what they get are three
dimensions—and comprehensible little packets of
time—and enclosures making possible the crucial
distinction between inside and outside.

There is no inside here. There is no outside
here. To pass through the gates in either direction
is to go from nowhere to nowhere and from
everywhere to everywhere. Imagine a billiard
table as long and broad as the Milky Way. Do
not omit the detail of its being a flawless slate
slab to which green felt has been glued. Imagine
a gate at dead center on the slab. Anyone
imagining that much will have comprehended all
there is to know about Paradise—and will have
sympathized with those becoming ravenous for
the distinction between inside and outside.

R

Uncomfortable as it is here, however, there are a
few of us who do not care to be reborn. I am among
that number. I have not been on Earth since 1587
A.D., when, riding around in the meat of one
Walpurga Hausmännin, I was executed in the
Austrian village of Dillingen. The alleged crime
of my meat was witchcraft. When I heard the
sentence, I certainly wanted out of that meat. I
was about to leave it anyway, having worn it for
more than eighty-five years. But I had to stay
right with it when they tied it astride a sawhorse,
put the sawhorse on a cart, took my poor old
meat to the Town Hall. There they tore my right
arm and left breast with red-hot pincers. Then

we went to the lower gate, where they tore my
right breast. Then they took me to the door of
the hospital, where they tore my right arm. And
that they took me to the village square. In view
of the fact that I had been a licensed and pledged
midwife for sixty-two years, and yet had acted so
vilely, they cut off my right hand. And then they
tied me to a stake, burned me alive, and dumped
my ashes into the nearest stream.

As I say, I haven't been back since.

R

It used to be that most of us who didn't want to
go back to good old Earth where souls whose meat
had been tortured in slow and fancy ways—a fact
that should make very smug indeed proponents
of corporal and capital punishments and deterrents
to crime. But something curious had been
happening of late. We have been gaining recruits
to whom, by our standards of agony, practically
nothing happened on Earth. They scarcely barked
a shin down there, and yet they arrive up here in
shell-shocked battalions, bawling, "Never again!"

"Who are these people?" I ask myself. "What
is this unimaginably horrible thing that has
happened to them??" And I realize that, in order
to get proper answers, I am going to have to
cease to be dead. I am going to have to let myself
be reborn.

Word has just come that I am to be sent where
the soul of Richard the Lion Hearted now lives,
Rosewater, Indiana.

Eliot's black telephone rang.

"This is the Rosewater Foundation. How can we help
you?"

"Mr. Rosewater—" said a woman chokingly, "this—

this is Stella Wakeby." She panted, waiting for his reaction to the announcement.

"Well! Hello!" said Eliot heartily. "How nice to *hear* from you! What a pleasant surprise!" He didn't know who Stella Wakeby was.

"Mr. Rosewater—I—I never asked you for anything, did I?"

"No—no, you never did."

"A lot of people with a lot less troubles than I got bother you all the time."

"I never feel that anyone is *bothering* me. It is true— I do see some people more than others." He did so much business with Diana Moon Glampers, for instance, that he no longer recorded his transactions with her in the book. He took a chance now: "And I've often thought of the awful burdens you must have to carry."

"Oh, Mr. Rosewater—if you only *knew*—" And she burst into violent tears. "We always said we were *Senator* Rosewater people and not *Eliot* Rosewater people!"

"There, there."

"We've always stood on our own two feet, no matter what. Many's the time I passed you out on the street and looked the other way, not on account of I had anything against you. I just wanted you to know the Wakebys were *fine*."

"I understood—and I was always glad to get the good news." Eliot couldn't recall any woman's turning her face away from him, and he walked around the town so rarely that he couldn't have offered the overwrought Stella very many opportunities to react to him. He supposed correctly that she lived in frightful poverty on some back road, rarely showing herself and her rags, and only imagining that she had some sort of life in the town, too, and that everyone knew her. If she had passed Eliot on the street once, which she probably had, that once had become a thousand passings in her mind— each with its own dramatic lights and shadows.

"I couldn't sleep tonight, Mr. Rosewater—so I walked the road."

"And many's the time you've done it."

"Oh, God, Mr. Rosewater—full moon, half moon, and no moon at all."

"And tonight the rain."

"I like the rain."

"And so do I."

"And there was this light in my neighbor's house."

"Thank God for neighbors."

"And I knocked on the door, and they took me in. And I said, 'I just can't go another step without some kind of help. If I can't get some kind of help. I don't care if tomorrow never comes. I can't be a Senator Rosewater person any more!' "

"There, there—now, now."

"So they put me in the car, and they drove me to the nearest telephone, and they said, 'You call up Eliot. He'll help.' So that's what I've *done*."

"Would you like to come see me now, dear—or can you wait until tomorrow?"

"Tomorrow." It was almost a question.

"Wonderful! Any time that's convenient to you, dear."

"Tomorrow."

"Tomorrow, dear. It's going to be a very nice day."

"Thank *God!*"

"There, there."

"Ohhhhh, Mr. Rosewater, thank God for *you!*"

R

Eliot hung up. The telephone rang immediately.

"This is the Rosewater Foundation. How can we help you?"

"You might start by getting a haircut and a new suit," said a man.

"What?"

"Eliot—"

"Yes—?"

"You don't even recognize my voice?"

"I—I'm sorry—I—"

"It's your God-damned *Dad!*"

R

"Gee, *Father!*" said Eliot, lyrical with love, surprise and pleasure. "How *nice* to hear your voice."

"You didn't even recognize it."

"Sorry. You know—the calls just *pour* in."

"They do, eh?"

"*You* know that."

"I'm afraid I do."

"Gee—how *are* you, anyway?"

"Fine!" said the Senator with brisk sarcasm. "Couldn't be better!"

"I'm so glad to hear that."

The Senator cursed.

"What's the matter, Father?"

"Don't talk to me as though I were some drunk! Some pimp! Some moronic washerwoman!"

"What did I *say?*"

"Your whole damn tone!"

"Sorry."

"I can sense your getting ready to tell me to take an aspirin in a glass of wine. Don't talk *down* to me!"

"Sorry."

"I don't need anybody to make the last payment on my motor scooter." Eliot had actually done this for a client once. The client killed himself and a girlfriend two days later, smashed up in Bloomington.

"I know you don't."

"He knows I don't," said the Senator to somebody on his end of the line.

"You—you sound so *angry* and *unhappy,* Father." Eliot was genuinely concerned.

"It will pass."

"Is it anything special?"

"Little things, Eliot, little things—such as the Rosewater family's dying out."

"What makes you think it *is?*"

"Don't tell me you're pregnant."

"What about the people in Rhode Island?"

"You make me feel so much better. I'd forgotten all about them."

"Now you sound sarcastic."

"It must be a bad connection. Tell me some good news from out your way, Eliot. Buoy up this old futz."

"Mary Moody had twins."

"Good! Good! Wonderful! As long as *somebody's* reproducing. And what names has Miss Moody chosen for these new little citizens?"

"Foxcroft and Melody."

R

"Eliot—"

"Sir—?"

"I want you to take a good look at yourself."

Dutifully, Eliot looked himself over as best he could without a mirror. "I'm looking."

"Now ask yourself, 'Is this a dream? How did I ever get into such a disreputable condition?' "

Again dutifully, and without a trace of whimsicality, Eliot said to himself out loud, "Is this a dream? How did I ever get into such a disreputable condition?"

"Well? What is your answer?"

"Isn't a dream," Eliot reported.

"Don't you wish it *were?*"

"What would I wake up *to?*"

"What you can *be*. What you *used* to be!"

"You want me to start buying paintings for museums again? Would you be prouder of me, if I'd contributed two and a half million dollars to buy Rembrandt's

Aristotle Contemplating a Bust of Homer?"

"Don't reduce the argument to an absurdity."

"I'm not the one who did *that*. Blame the people who put up that kind of money for that kind of picture. I showed a photograph of it to Diana Moon Glampers, and she said, 'Maybe I'm dumb, Mr. Rosewater, but I wouldn't give that thing house room.' "

"Eliot—"

"Sir—?"

"Ask yourself what Harvard would think of you now."

"I don't have to. I already know."

"Oh?"

"They're crazy about me. You should see the letters I get."

The Senator nodded to himself resignedly, knowing that the Harvard jibe was ill-considered, knowing Eliot told the truth when he spoke of letters from Harvard that were full of respect.

"After all—"said Eliot, "for goodness sakes, I've given those guys three hundred thousand dollars a year, regular as clockwork, ever since the Foundation began. You should *see* the letters."

R

"Eliot—"

"Sir—?"

"We come to a supremely ironic moment in history, for Senator Rosewater of Indiana now asks his own son, 'Are you or have you ever been a communist?' "

"Oh, I have what a lot of people would probably call communistic thoughts," said Eliot artlessly, "but, for heaven's sakes, Father, nobody can work with the poor and not fall over Karl Marx from time to time—or just fall over the Bible, as far as that goes. I think it's terrible the way people don't share things in this country. I think it's a heartless government that will let one baby be born owning a big piece of the country, the way I was born, and let another baby be born without owning anything. The least a government could do, it seems to me, is to divide things up fairly among the babies. Life is hard enough, without people having to worry themselves sick about *money,* too. There's plenty for everybody in this country, if we'll only *share* more."

"And just what do you think that would do to incentive?"

"You mean fright about not getting enough to eat, about not being able to pay the doctor, about not being able to give your family nice clothes, a safe, cheerful, comfortable place to live, a decent education, and a few good times? You mean shame about not knowing where the Money River is?"

"The *what?*"

"The Money River, where the wealth of the nation flows. We were born on the banks of it—and so were most of the mediocre people we grew up with, went to private schools with, sailed and played tennis with. We can slurp from that mighty river to our hearts' content. And we even take slurping lessons, so we can slurp more efficiently."

"Slurping lessons?"

"From lawyers! From tax consultants! From customers' men! We're born close enough to to the river to drown ourselves and the next ten generations in wealth, simply using dippers and buckets. But we still hire the experts to teach us the use of aqueducts, dams, reservoirs, siphons, bucket brigades, and the Archimedes' screw. And our teachers in turn become rich, and their children become buyers of lessons in slurping."

"I wasn't aware that I slurped."

Eliot was fleetingly heartless, for he was thinking angrily in the abstract. "Born slurpers never are. And they can't imagine what the poor people are talking about when they say they hear somebody slurping. They don't even know what it means when somebody

mentions the Money River. When one of us claims that
there is no such thing as the Money River I think to
myself, 'My gosh, but that's a dishonest and tasteless
thing to say.' "

R

"How stimulating to hear you talk of taste," said
the Senator clankingly.

"You want me to start going to the opera again?
You want me to build a perfect house in a perfect
village, and sail and sail and sail?"

"Who cares what I want?"

"I admit this is no Taj Mahal. But should it be, with
other Americans having such a rotten time?"

"Perhaps, if they stopped believing in crazy things
like the Money River, and got to work, they would stop
having such a rotten time."

"If there isn't a Money River, then how did I make
ten thousand dollars today, just by snoozing and
scratching myself, and occasionally answering the
phone?"

"It's still possible for an American to make a fortune
on his own."

"Sure—provided somebody tells him when he's young
enough that there *is* a Money River, that there's nothing
fair about it, that he had damn well better forget about
hard work and the merit system and honesty and all
that crap, and get to where the river is. 'Go where the
rich and the powerful are,' I'd tell him, 'and learn their
ways. They can be flattered and they can be scared.
Please them enormously or scare them enormously, and
one moonless night they will put their fingers to their
lips, warning you not to make a sound. And they will
lead you through the dark to the widest, deepest river
of wealth ever known to man. You'll be shown your
place on the riverbank, and handed a bucket all your
own. Slurp as much as you want, but try to keep the

racket of your slurping down. A poor man might hear.' "

The Senator cursed.

"Why did you say that, Father?" It was a tender question.

The Senator cursed again.

"I just wish there didn't have to be this *arcrimony*, this tension, every time we talk. I love you so."

There was more cursing, made harsher by the fact that the Senator was close to tears.

"Why would you swear when I say I love you, Father?"

"You're the man who stands on a street corner with a roll of toilet paper, and written on each square are the words, 'I love you.' And each passer-by, no matter who, gets a square all his or her own. I don't want *my* square of toilet paper."

"I didn't realize it *was* toilet paper."

"Until you stop drinking, you're not going to realize anything!" the Senator cried brokenly. "I'm going to put your wife on the phone. Do you realize you've lost her? Do you realize what a good wife she was?"

R

"Eliot—?" Sylvia's was such a breathy and frightened greeting. The girl weighed no more than a wedding veil.

"Sylvia—" This was formal, manly, but even. Eliot had written to her a thousand times, had called and called. Until now, there had been no reply.

"I—I am aware that—that I have behaved badly."

"As long as the behavior was human—"

"Can I help being human?"

"No."

"Can anybody?"

"Not that I know of."

R

"Eliot—?"
  "Yes?"
  "How is everybody?"
  "Here?"
  "Anywhere."
  "Fine."
  "I'm glad."

R

"If—if I ask about certain people, I'll cry," said Sylvia.
  "Don't ask."
  "I still care about them, even if the doctors tell me I mustn't ever go there again."
  "Don't ask."
  "Somebody had a baby?"
  "Don't ask."
  "Didn't you tell your father somebody had a baby?"
  "Don't ask."
  "Who had a baby, Eliot?—I care, I care."
  "Oh Christ, don't ask."
  "I care, I care!"
  "Mary Moody."
  "Twins?"
  "Of course." Eliot revealed here that he had no illusions about the people to whom he was devoting his life. "And firebugs, too, no doubt, no doubt." The Moody family had a long history of not only twinning but arson.
  "Are they cute?"
  "I haven't seen them." Eliot added with an irritability that had always been a private thing between himself and Sylvia. "They always are."
  "Have you sent their presents yet?"
  "What makes you think I still send presents?" This

had reference to Eliot's old custom of sending a share of International Business Machines stock to each child born in the county.

"You don't do it any more?"

"I still do it." Eliot sounded sick of doing it.

"You seem tired."

"It must be a bad connection."

"Tell me some more news."

"My wife is divorcing me for medical reasons."

"Can't we skip that news?" This was not a flippant suggestion. It was a tragic one. The tragedy was beyond discussion.

"Hippity hop," said Eliot emptily.

R

Eliot took a drink of Southern Comfort, was uncomforted. He coughed, and his father coughed, too. This coincidence, where father and son matched each other unknowingly, inconsolable hack for hack, was heard not only by Sylvia, but by Norman Mushari, too. Mushari had slipped out of the living room, had found a telephone extension in the Senator's study. He was listening in with ears ablaze.

"I—I suppose I should say goodbye," said Sylvia guiltily. Tears were streaming down her cheeks.

"That would be up to your doctor to say."

"Give—give my love to everyone."

"I will, I will."

"Tell them I dream about them all the time."

"That will make them proud."

"Congratulate Mary Moody on her twins."

"I will. I'll be baptizing them tomorrow."

"Baptizing?" This was something new.

Mushari rolled his eyes.

"I—I didn't know you—you did things like that," said Sylvia carefully.

Mushari was gratified to hear the anxiety in her

voice. It meant to him that Eliot's lunacy was not stabilized, but was about to make the great leap forward into religion.

"I couldn't get out of it," said Eliot. "She insisted on it, and nobody else would do it."

"Oh." Sylvia relaxed.

Mushari did not register disappointment. The baptism would hold up very well in court as evidence that Eliot thought of himself as a Messiah.

"I told her," said Eliot, and Mushari's mind, which was equipped with ratchets, declined to accept this evidence, "that I wasn't a religious person by any stretch of the imagination. I told her nothing I did would count in Heaven, but she insisted just the same."

"What will you say? What will you do?"

"Oh—I don't know." Eliot's sorrow and exhaustion dropped away for a moment as he became enchanted by the problem. A birdy little smile played over his lips. "Go over to her shack, I guess. Sprinkle some water on the babies, say, 'Hello, babies. Welcome to Earth. It's hot in the summer and cold in the winter. It's round and wet and crowded. At the outside, babies, you've got about a hundred years here. There's only one rule that I know of, babies—:

" 'God damn it, you've got to be kind.' "

8.

IT WAS AGREED that night that Eliot and Sylvia should meet for a final farewell in the Bluebird Room of the Marott Hotel in Indianapolis, three nights hence. This was a tremendously dangerous thing for two such sick and loving people to do. The agreement was reached in a chaos of murmurs and whispers and little cries of loneliness that came at the close of the telephone conversation.

"Oh, Eliot, should we?"

"I think we have to."

"Have to," she echoed.

"Don't you feel it—that—that we have to?"

"Yes."

"It's life."

Sylvia wagged her head. "Oh, damn love—damn love."

"This will be nice. I promise."

"I promise, too."

"I'll get a new suit."

"Please don't—not on my account."

"On account of the Bluebird Room, then."

"Good night."

"I love you, Sylvia. Good night."

There was a pause.

"Good night, Eliot."

"I love you."

"Good night. I'm frightened. Good night."

R

This conversation was a worry to Norman Mushari, who restored the telephone with which he had been eaves-dropping to its cradle. It was crucial to his plans that Sylvia not get pregnant by Eliot. A child in her womb would have an unbreakable claim to control of the Foundation, whether Eliot was crazy or not. And it was Mushari's dream that control should go to Eliot's second cousin, Fred Rosewater, in Pisquontuit, Rhode Island.

Fred knew nothing of this, didn't even know for certain that he was related to the Indiana Rosewaters. The Indiana Rosewaters knew about him only because McAllister, Robjent, Reed and McGee, being thorough, had hired a genealogist and a detective to find out who their closest relatives bearing the name Rosewater were. Fred's dossier in the law firm's confidential files was fat, as was Fred, but the investigation had been discreet. Fred never imagined that he might be tapped for wealth and glory.

R

So, on the morning after Eliot and Sylvia agreed to meet, Fred felt like an ordinary or less-than-ordinary man, whose prospects were poor. He came out of the Pisquontuit Drug Store, squinted in the sunlight, took three deep breaths, went into the Pisquontuit News Store next door. He was a portly man, aslop with coffee, gravid with Danish pastry.

Poor, lugubrious Fred spent his mornings seeking insurance prospects in the drugstore, which was the coffee house of the rich, and the news store, which

was the coffee house of the poor. He was the only man
in town who had coffee in *both* places.

Fred bellied up to the news store's lunch counter,
beamed at a carpenter and two plumbers sitting there.
He climbed aboard a stool, and his great behind made
the cushion seem no larger than a marshmallow.

"Coffee and Danish, Mr. Rosewater?" said the
not-very-clean idiot girl behind the counter.

"Coffee and Danish sounds real good," Fred agreed
heartily. "On a morning like this, by God, coffee and
Danish sounds real good."

R

About Pisquontuit: It was pronounced "Pawn-it" by
those who loved it, and "Piss-on-it" by those who didn't.
There had once been an Indian chief named Pisquontuit.

Pisquontuit wore an apron, lived, as did his people,
on clams, raspberries, and rose hips. Agriculture
was news to Chief Pisquontuit. So, for that matter, were
wampum, feather ornaments, and the bow and arrow.

Alcohol was the best news of all. Pisquontuit drank
himself to death in 1638.

Four thousand moons later, the village that made his
name immortal was populated by two hundred very
wealthy families and by a thousand ordinary families
whose breadwinners served, in one way and another,
the rich.

The lives led there were nearly all paltry, lacking in
subtlety, wisdom, wit or invention—were precisely as
pointless and unhappy as lives led in Rosewater, Indiana.
Inherited millions did not help. Nor did the arts and
sciences.

R

Fred Rosewater was a good sailor and had attended
Princeton University, so he was welcomed into the

homes of the rich, though, for Pisquontuit, he was gruesomely poor. His home was a sordid little brown-shingle carpenter's special, a mile from the glittering waterfront.

Poor Fred worked like hell for the few dollars he brought home once in a while. He was working now, beaming at the carpenter and the two plumbers in the news store. The three workmen were reading a scandalous tabloid, a national weekly dealing with murder, sex, pets, and children—*mutilated* children, more often than not. It was called *The American Investigator*, "The World's Most Sparkling Newspaper." *The Investigator* was to the news store what *The Wall Street Journal* was to the drugstore.

"Improving your minds as usual, I see," Fred observed. He said it with the lightness of fruitcake.

The workmen had an uneasy respect for Fred. They tried to be cynical about what he sold, but they knew in their hearts that he was offering the only get-rich-quick scheme that was open to them: to insure themselves and die soon. And it was Fred's gloomy secret that without such people, tantalized by such a proposition, he would not have a dime. All of his business was with the working class. His cavorting with the sailboat rajahs next door was bluster, bluff. It impressed the poor to think that Fred sold insurance to the canny rich, too, but it was not true. The estate plans of the rich were made in banks and law offices far, far away.

"What's the foreign news today?" Fred inquired. This was another joke about *The Investigator*.

The carpenter held up the front page for Fred to see. The page was well filled by a headline and a picture of a fine looking young woman. The headline said this:

**I WANT A MAN WHO
CAN GIVE ME A
GENIUS BABY!**

The girl was a showgirl. Her name was Randy Herald.

"I'd be *pleased* to help the lady with her problem," said Fred, lightly again.

"My God," said the carpenter, cocking his head and gnashing his teeth, "wouldn't anybody?"

"You think I'm *serious?*" Fred sneered at Randy Herald. "I wouldn't trade my bride for twenty thousand Randy Heralds!" He was calculatingly maudlin now. "And I don't think you guys would trade *your* brides, either." To Fred, a bride was any woman with an insurable husband.

"I know your brides," he continued, "and any one of you would be crazy to trade." He nodded. "We are four lucky guys sitting here, and we'd better not forget it. Four wonderful brides we've got, boys, and we'd damn well better stop and thank God for 'em from time to time."

Fred stirred his coffee. "I wouldn't be anything without my bride, and I know it." His bride was named Caroline. Caroline was the mother of an unattractive, fat little boy, poor little Franklin Rosewater. Caroline had taken lately to drinking lunch with a rich Lesbian named Amanita Buntline.

"I've done what I can for her," Fred declared. "God knows it isn't enough. Nothing could be enough." There was a real lump in his throat. He knew that lump had to be there and it had to be real, or he wouldn't sell any insurance. "It's something, though, something even a poor man can do for his bride."

Fred rolled his eyes mooningly. He was worth forty-two thousand dollars dead.

R

Fred was often asked, of course, whether he was related to the famous Senator Rosewater. Fred's self-effacing, ignorant reply was along the lines of, "Somewhere, somehow, I guess—way, way back." Like most

Americans of modest means, Fred knew nothing about his ancestors.

There was this to know:

The Rhode Island branch of the Rosewater family was descended from George Rosewater, younger brother of the infamous Noah. When the Civil War came, George raised a company of Indiana riflemen, marched off with them to join the nearly legendary *Black Hat Brigade*. Under George's command was Noah's substitute, the Rosewater village idiot, Fletcher Moon. Moon was blown to hamburger by Stonewall Jackson's artillery at Second Bull Run.

During the retreat through the mud toward Alexandria, Captain Rosewater took time out to write his brother Noah this note:

> Fletcher Moon kept up his end of the deal to the utmost of his ability. If you are put out about your considerable investment in him being used up so quickly, I suggest you write General Pope for a partial refund. Wish you were here.
>
> George

To which Noah replied:

> I am sorry about Fletcher Moon, but, as the *Bible* says, "A deal is a deal" Enclosed find some routine legal papers for you to sign. They empower me to run your half of the farm and the saw factory until you return, etc., etc. We are undergoing great privations here at home. Everything is goings to the troops. A word of appreciation from the troops would be much appreciated.
>
> Noah.

By the time of Antietam, George Rosewater had become a Lieutenant Colonel, and had, curiously, lost

the little fingers from both hands. At Antietam, he had
his horse shot out from under him, advanced on foot,
grabbed the regimental colors from a dying boy, found
himself holding only a shattered staff when Confederate
cannister carried the colors away. He pressed on,
killed a man with the staff. At the moment he was doing
the killing, one of his own men fired off a musket that
still had its ramrod jammed down the bore. The
explosion blinded Colonel Rosewater for life.

        R

George returned to Rosewater County a blind brevet
brigadier. People found him remarkably cheerful. And
his cheerfulness did not seem to fade one iota when it
was explained to him by bankers and lawyers, who
kindly offered to be his eyes, that he didn't own
anything any more, that he had signed everything over
to Noah. Noah, unfortunately, was not in town to
explain things in person to George. Business required
that he spend most of his time in Washington, New
York and Philadelphia.

"Well," said George, still smiling, smiling, smiling,
"as the Bible tells us in no uncertain terms, 'Business is
business.' "

The lawyers and bankers felt somewhat cheated,
since George didn't seem to be drawing any sort of
moral from what should have been an important
experience in almost any man's life. One lawyer, who
had been looking forward to pointing out the moral
when George got mad, couldn't restrain himself from
pointing it out anyway, even though George was
laughing: "People should always *read* things before they
sign them."

"You can bet your boots," said George, "that from
now on I *will*."

George Rosewater obviously wasn't a well man when

he came back from the war, for no well man, having
lost his eyes and his patrimony, would have laughed so
much. And a well man, particularly if he were a general
and a hero, might have taken some vigorous legal steps
to compel his brother to return his property. But George
filed no suit. He did not wait for Noah to return to
Rosewater County, and he did not go East to find him.
In fact, he and Noah were never to meet or
communicate again.

He paid a call, wearing the full regalia of a brigadier,
to each Rosewater County household that had given
him a boy or boys to command, praising them all,
mourning with all his heart for the boys who were
wounded or dead. Noah Rosewater's brick mansion
was being built at that time. One morning the workmen
found the brigadier's uniform nailed to the front
door as though it were an animal skin nailed to a barn
door to dry.

As far as Rosewater County was concerned, George
Rosewater had disappeared forever.

R

George went East like a vagabond, not to find and kill
his brother, but to seek work in Providence, Rhode
Island. He had heard that a broom factory was being
opened there. It was to be staffed by Union veterans
who were blind.

What he had heard was true. There was such a
factory founded by Castor Buntline, who was neither
a veteran nor blind. Buntline perceived correctly that
blind veterans would make very agreeable employees,
that Buntline himself would gain a place in history
as a humanitarian, and that no Northern patriot, for
several years after the war, anyway, would use anything
but a *Buntline Union Beacon Broom*. Thus was the
great Buntline fortune begun. And, with broom profits,

Castor Buntline and his spastic son Elihu went
carpetbagging, became tobacco kings.

R

When the footsore, amiable General George Rosewater
arrived at the broom factory, Castor Buntline wrote to
Washington, confirmed that George was a general,
hired George at a very good salary, made him foreman,
and named the whiskbrooms the factory was making
after him. The brand name entered ordinary speech for
a little while. A "General Rosewater" was a *whiskbroom*.

And blind George was given a fourteen-year-old girl,
an orphan named Faith Merrihue, who was to be his
eyes and his messenger. When she was sixteen, George
married her.

And George begat Abraham, who became a
Congregationalist minister. Abraham went as a
missionary to the Congo, where he met and married
Lavinia Waters, the daughter of another missionary, an
Illinois Baptist.

In the jungle, Abraham begat Merrihue. Lavinia
died at Merrihue's birth. Little Merrihue was nursed
on the milk of a Bantu.

And Abraham and little Merrihue returned to Rhode
Island. Abraham accepted the call to the
Congregationalist pulpit in the little fishing village of
Pisquontuit. He bought a little house, and with that
house came one hundred ten acres of scruffy, sandy
woodlot. It was a triangular lot. The hypotenuse of
the triangle lay on the shore of Pisquontuit Harbor.

Merrihue, the Parson's son, became a realtor,
divided his father's lands into lots. He married Cynthia
Niles Rumfoord, a minor heiress, invested much of her
money in pavement and streetlights and sewers. He
made a fortune, lost it, and his wife's fortune, too, in
the crash of 1929.

He blew his brains out.

But before, he did that, he wrote a family history and he begat poor Fred, the insurance man.

R

Sons of suicides seldom do well.

Characteristically, they find life lacking a certain *zing*. They tend to feel more rootless than most, even in a notoriously rootless nation. They are squeamishly incurious about the past and numbly certain about the future to this grisly extent: they suspect that they, too, will probably kill themselves.

The syndrome was surely Fred's. And to it he added twitches, aversions and listlessnesses special to his own case. He had heard the shot that killed his father, had seen his father with a big piece of his head blown away, with the manuscript of the family history in his lap.

Fred had the manuscript, which he had never read, which he never wanted to read. It was on top of a jelly cupboard in the cellar of Fred's home. That was where he kept the rat poison, too.

R

Now poor Fred Rosewater was in the news store, continuing to talk to the carpenter and the two plumbers about brides. "Ned—" he said to the carpenter, *"we've* both done something for our brides, anyway." The carpenter was worth twenty thousand dollars dead, thanks to Fred. He could think of little else but suicide whenever premium time rolled around.

"And we can forget all about saving, too," said Fred. "That's all taken care of—*automatically.*"

"Yup," said Ned.

There was a waterlogged silence. The two uninsured

plumbers, gay and lecherous moments before, were lifeless now.

"With a simple stroke of the pen," Fred reminded the carpenter, "we've created sizable estates. That's the miracle of life insurance. That's the least we can do for our brides."

The plumbers slid off their stools. Fred was not dismayed as to see them go. They would be taking their consciences with them wherever they went—and they would be coming back to the news store again and again.

And whenever they came back, there would be Fred.

"You know what my greatest satisfaction is in my profession?" Fred asked the carpenter.

"Nope."

"It comes when I have a bride come up to me and say, 'I don't know how the children and I can ever thank you enough for what you've done. God bless you, Mr. Rosewater.' "

9.

THE CARPENTER slunk away from Fred Rosewater, too, leaving a copy of *The American Investigator* behind. Fred went through an elaborate pantomime of ennui, demonstrated to anyone who might be watching that he was a man with absolutely nothing to read, a sleepy man, possible hung over, and that he was likely to seize any reading matter at all, like a man in a dream.

"Uff, uff, uff," he yawned. He stretched out his arms, gathered the paper in.

There seemed to be only one other person in the store, the girl behind the lunch counter. "Really now—" he said to her, "who are the idiots who read this garbage, anyway?"

The girl might have responded truthfully that Fred himself read it from cover to cover every week. But, being an idiot herself, she noticed practically nothing. "Search me," she said.

It was an unappetizing invitation.

R

Fred Rosewater, snorting with incredulity, turned to the advertising section of the paper, which was called,

"Here I Am." Men and women confessed there that
they were looking for love, marriage, and monkeyshines.
They did so at a cost to themselves of a dollar forty-five
cents per line.

> Attractive, sparkling, professional woman, 40,
> Jewish, *said one,* college graduate, resides
> Connecticut. Seeks marriage-minded Jewish
> college-educated man. Children warmly welcomed.
> Investigator, Box L-577.

That was a sweet one. Most weren't that sweet.

> St. Louis hairdresser, male, would like to hear
> from other males in Show-me State. Exchange
> snaps? *said another.*
> Modern couple new to Dallas would like to
> meet sophisticated couples interested in candid
> photography. All sincere letters answered. All
> snaps returned, *said another.*
> Male preparatory school teacher badly needs
> course in manners from stern instructress,
> preferably a horse-lover of German or Scandinavian
> extraction, *said another.* Will travel anywhere
> in U.S.
> New York top exec wants dates weekday
> afternoons. No prudes, *said another.*

On the facing page was a large coupon on which a
reader was invited to write an ad of his own. Fred sort
of hankered to.

R

Fred turned the page, read an account of a rape-murder
that happened in Nebraska in 1933. The illustrations
were revoltingly clinical photographs that only a coroner
had a right to see. The rape-murder was thirty years

old when Fred read of it, when *The Investigator's*
reputedly ten million readers read of it. The issues
with which the paper dealt were eternal. Lucretia Borgia
could make screaming headlines at any time. It was
from *The Investigator,* in fact, that Fred, who had
attended Princeton for only a year, had learned of the
death of Socrates.

A thirteen-year-old girl came into the store, and Fred
thrust the paper aside. The girl was Lila Buntline,
daughter of his wife's best friend. Lila was a tall
creature, horse-faced, knobby. They were great circles
under her perfectly beautiful green eyes. Her face was
piebald with sunburn and tan and freckles and pink new
skin. She was the most competitive and skilful sailor
in the Pisquontuit Yacht Club.

Lila glanced at Fred with pity—because he was poor,
because his wife was no good, because he was fat,
because he was a bore. And she strode to the magazine
and book racks, put herself out of sight by sitting on the
cold cement floor.

Fred retrieved *The Investigator,* looked at ads that
offered to sell him all sorts of dirty things. His breathing
was shallow. Poor Fred had a damp, junior high school
enthusiasm for *The Investigator* and all it stood for,
but lacked the nerve to become a part of it, to correspond
with all the box numbers there. Since he was the son
of a suicide, it was hardly surprising that his secret
hankerings were embarrassing and small.

R

A very healthy man now banged into the news store,
moved to Fred's side so quickly that Fred couldn't throw
the paper away. "Why, you filthy-minded insurance
bastard," said the newcomer cheerfully, "what you
doing reading a jerk-off paper like that?"

He was Harry Pena, a professional fisherman. He
was also Chief of the Pisquontuit Volunteer Fire

Department. Harry had two fish traps offshore, labyrinths
of pilings and nets that took heartless advantage of the
stupidity of fish. Each trap was a long fence in the
water, with dry land at one end and a circular corral
of stakes and netting at the other. Fish seeking a way
way around the fence entered the corral. Stupidly, they
circled the corral again and again and again, until Harry
and his two big sons came in their boat, with gaffhooks
and malls, closed the gate of the corral, hauled up a
purse net lying on the bottom, and killed and killed
and killed.

Harry was middle-aged and bandy-legged, but he had
a head and shoulders Michelangelo might have given
to Moses or God. He had not been a fisherman all his
life. Harry had been an insurance bastard himself, in
Pittsfield, Massachusetts. One night in Pittsfield, Harry
had cleaned his living-room carpet with carbon
tetrachloride, and all but died. When he recovered his
doctor told him this: "Harry—either you work
out-of-doors, or you die."

So Harry became what his father had been—a trap
fisherman.

R

Harry threw an arm over Fred's suety shoulders. He
could afford to be affectionate. He was one of the few
men in Pisquontuit whose manhood was not in question.
"Aaaaah—you poor insurance bastard—" he said, "why
be an insurance bastard? Do something beautiful." He
sat down, ordered black coffee and a golden cigar.

"Well now, Harry—" said Fred, with lip-pursing
judiciousness, "I think maybe my insurance philosophy
is a little different from what yours was."

"Shit," said Harry pleasantly. He took the paper
away from Fred, considered the front-page challenge
hurled by Randy Herald. "By God," he said, "she takes

whatever kind of baby I give her, and I say *when* she gets it, too, not her."

"Seriously, Harry—" Fred insisted, "I *like* insurance. I like *helping* people."

Harry gave no indication that he'd heard. He scowled at a picture of a French girl in a bikini.

Fred, understanding that he seemed a bleak, sexless person to Harry, tried to prove that Harry had him wrong. He nudged Harry, man-to-man. "Like that, Harry?" he asked.

"Like what?"

"The girl there."

"That's not a girl. That's a piece of paper."

"Looks like a girl to *me*." Fred Rosewater leered.

"Then you're easily fooled," said Harry. "It's done with ink on a piece of paper. That girl isn't lying there on the counter. She's thousand of miles away, doesn't even know we're alive. If this was a real girl, all I'd have to do for a living would be to stay home and cut out pictures of big fish.'"

R

Harry Pena turned to the "Here I Am" ads, asked Fred for a pen.

"Pen?" said Fred Rosewater, as though it were a foreign word.

"You've *got* one, don't you?"

"Sure, I've got one." Fred handed over one of the nine pens distributed about his person.

"Sure he's got one." Harry laughed. And this is what he wrote on the coupon facing the ads:

> Red-hot Papa, member of white race, seeks red-hot Mama, any race, any age, any religion. Object: everything but matrimony. Will exchange snaps. My teeth are my own.

"You really going to send that in?" Fred's own itch
to run an ad, to get a few dirty replies, was pathetically
plain.

Harry signed the ad: *"Fred Rosewater, Pisquontuit,
Rhode Island."*

"Very funny," said Fred, drawing back from Harry
with acid dignity.

Harry winked. "Funny for Pisquontuit," he said.

R

Fred's wife Caroline came into the news store now.
She was a pretty, pinched, skinny, lost little woman,
all dolled-up in well-made clothes cast off by her
wealthy, Lesbian friend, Amanita Buntline. Caroline
Rosewater clinked and flashed with accessories. Their
purpose was to make the second-hand clothing
distinctly her own. She was going to have lunch with
Amanita. She wanted money from Fred, in order that
she might insist, with something behind her, upon
paying for her own food and drink.

When she spoke to Fred, with Harry Pena watching,
she behaved like a woman who was keeping her dignity
while being frog-walked. With the avid help of Amanita,
she pitied herself for being married to a man who was
so poor and dull. That she was exactly as poor and dull as
Fred was a possibility she was constitutionally unable to
entertain. For one thing, she was a Phi Beta Kappa,
having won her key as a philosophy major at Dillon
University, in Dodge City, Kansas. That was where
she and Fred had met, in Dodge City, in a U.S.O. Fred
had been stationed at Fort Riley during the Korean
War. She married Fred because she thought everybody
who lived in Pisquontuit and had been to Princeton
was rich.

She was humiliated to discover that it was not true.
She honestly believed that she was an intellectual, but
she knew almost nothing, and every problem she ever

considered could be solved by just one thing: money, and lots of it. She was a frightful housekeeper. She cried when she did housework, because she was convinced that she was cut out for better things.

As for the Lesbian business, it wasn't particularly deep on Caroline's part. She was simply a female chameleon trying to get ahead in the world.

R

"Lunch with Amanita again?" Fred whinnied.

"Why not?"

"This gets to be damn expensive, fancy lunches every day."

"It isn't every day. It's twice a week at the very most." She was brittle and cold.

"It's still a hell of an expense, Caroline."

Caroline held out a white-gloved hand for money. "It's worth it to your wife."

Fred gave her money.

Caroline did not thank Fred. She left, took her place on a fawn-colored cushion of glove leather, next to the fragrant Amanita Buntline in Amanita's powder-blue Mercedes *300-SL.*

Harry Pena looked at Fred's chalky face appraisingly. He made no comment. He lit a cigar, departed—went fishing for real fish with his two real sons—in a real boat on a salty sea.

R

Lila, the daughter of Amanita Buntline, sat on the cold floor of the news store, reading Henry Miller's *Tropic of Cancer,* which, along with William Burrough's *Naked Lunch,* she had taken from the Lazy Susan book rack. Lila's interest in the books was commercial. At thirteen, she was Pisquontuit's leading dealer in smut.

She was a dealer in fireworks, too, for the same

reason she was a dealer in smut, which was: *Profit*.
Her playmates at the Pisquontuit Yacht Club and
Pisquontuit Country Day School were so rich and
foolish that they would pay her almost anything for
almost anything. In a routine business day, she might
sell a seventy-five-cent copy of *Lady Chatterley's Lover*
for ten dollars and fifteen-cent cherry bomb for five.

She bought her fireworks during family vacations
in Canada and Florida and Hong Kong. Most of her
smut came from the open stock of the news store. The
thing was, Lila knew which titles were red hot, which
was more than her playmates or the employees of the
news store knew. And Lila bought the hot ones as fast
as they were tucked into the Lazy Susan. All her
transactions were with the idiot behind the lunch counter,
who forgot everything faster than it could happen.

The relationship between Lila and the news store
was wonderfully symbiotic, for hanging in the store's
front window was a large medallion of gilded
polystyrene, awarded by the *Rhode Island Mothers to
Save Children from Filth*. Representatives of that group
inspected the store's paperback selection regularly.
The polystyrene medallion was their admission that they
had not found one filthy thing.

They thought that their children were safe, but the
truth was that Lila had cornered the market.

There was one sort of smut that Lila could not buy
at the news store—dirty pictures. She got them by doing
what Fred Rosewater had so often lusted weakly to do—
by answering raunchy ads in *The American Investigator*.

R

Large feet now intruded into her childish world on
the news store floor. They were the feet of Fred
Rosewater.

Lila did not conceal her red-hot books. She went on
reading, as though *The Tropic of Cancer* were *Heidi*:

The trunk is open and her things are lying around everywhere just as before. She lies down on the bed with her clothes on. Once, twice, three times, four times . . . I'm afraid she'll go mad . . . in bed, under the blankets, how good to feel her body again! But for how long? Will it last this time? Already I have a presentiment that it won't.

Lila and Fred often met between the books and magazines. Fred never asked her what she was reading. And she knew he would do what he always did—would look with sad hunger at the covers of girly magazines, then pick up and open something as fat and domestic as *Better Homes and Gardens*. This is precisely what he did now.

"I guess my wife is out to lunch with your Mummy again," said Fred.

"I guess she is," said Lila. That ended the conversation, but Lila continued to think about Fred. She was on level with the Rosewaters shins. She thought about them. Whenever she saw Fred in shorts or a bathing suit, his shins were covered with scars and scabs, as though he had been kicked and kicked and kicked every day of his life. Lila thought that maybe it was a vitamin deficiency that made Fred's shins look like that, or mange.

R

Fred's gory shins were victims of his wife's interior decorating scheme, which called for an almost schizophrenic use of little tables, dozens of them all through the house. Each little table had its own ashtray and dish of dusty after-dinner mints, although the Rosewaters never entertained. And Caroline was forever rearranging the tables, as though for this kind of party one day and another the next. So poor Fred was forever barking his shins on the tables.

One time Fred had had a deep cut on his chin that required eleven stitches. That fall hadn't been caused by all the little tables. It had been caused by an object that Caroline never put away. The object was always in evidence, like a pet anteater with a penchant for sleeping in doorways or on the staircase, or on the hearth.

That object, the one Fred had fallen over and cut his chin on, was Caroline Rosewater's *Electrolux*. Subconsciously, Caroline had sworn to herself that she would never put the vacuum cleaner away until she was rich.

R

Fred, thinking Lila wasn't paying any attention to him, now put down *Better Homes and Gardens,* picked up what looked like one hell of a sexy paperback novel, *Venus on the Half-shell,* by Kilgore Trout. On the back cover was an abridgment of a red-hot scene inside. It went like this:

> Queen Margaret of the planet Shaltoon let her gown fall to the floor. She was wearing nothing underneath. Her high, firm, uncowled bosom was proud and rosy. Her hips and thighs were like an inviting lyre of pure alabaster. They shone so whitely they might have had a light inside. 'Your travels are over, Space Wanderer,' she whispered, her voice husky with lust. 'Seek no more, for you have found. The answer is in my arms.'
>
> 'It's a glorious answer, Queen Margaret, God knows,' the Space Wanderer replied. His palms were perspiring profusely. 'I am going to accept it gratefully. But I have to tell you, if I'm going to be perfectly honest with you, that I will have to be on my way again tomorrow.'
>
> 'But you have found your answer, you have

found your answer,' she cried, and she forced his head between her fragrant young breasts.

He said something that she did not hear. She thrust him out at arm's length. 'What was that you said?'

'I said, Queen Margaret, that what you offer is an awfully good answer. It just doesn't happen to be the one I'm primarily looking for.'

There was a photograph of Trout. He was an old man with a full black beard. He looked like a frightened, aging Jesus, whose sentence to crucifixion had been commuted to imprisonment for life.

10.

LILA BUNTLINE peddled her bicycle through the muffled beauty of Pisquontuit's Utopian lanes. Every house she passed was a very expensive dream come true. The owners of the houses did not have to work at all. Neither would their children have to work, nor want for a thing, unless somebody revolted. Nobody seemed about to.

Lila's handsome house was on the harborfront. It was Georgian. She went inside, put down her new books in the hallway, stole into her father's study to make certain that her father, who was lying on his couch, was still alive. It was a thing she did at least once every day.

"Father—?"

The morning's mail was on a silver platter on a table at his head. Next to it was an untouched Scotch and soda. Its bubbles were dead. Stewart Buntline wasn't forty yet. He was the best looking man in town, a cross, somebody once said, between Cary Grant and a German shepherd. On his lean midsection lay a fifty-seven-dollar book, a railroad atlas of the Civil War, which his wife had given to him. That was his only enthusiasm in life, the Civil War.

"Daddy—"

Stewart snoozed on. His father had left him fourteen million dollars, tobacco money mostly. That money, churned and fertilized and hybridized and transmogrified in the hydroponic money farm of the Trust Department of the New England Seafarer's Bank and Trust Company of Boston, had increased by about eight hundred thousand dollars a year since it had been put in Stewart's name. Business seemed to be pretty good. Other than that, Stewart didn't know much about business.

Sometimes, when pressed to give his business views, he would declare roundly that he liked *Polaroid*. People seemed to find this vivid, that he should like *Polaroid* so much. Actually, he didn't know if he owned any *Polaroid* or not. The bank took care of things like that— the bank and the law firm of McAllister, Robjent, Reed and McGee.

"Daddy—"

"Mf?"

"I wanted to make sure you—you were all right," said Lila.

"Yup," he said. He couldn't be positive about it. He opened his eyes a little, licked his dry lips. "Fine, Sweetheart."

"You can go back to sleep now.'"

Stewart did.

R

There was no reason for him not to sleep soundly, for he was represented by the same law firm that represented Senator Rosewater, and had been since he was orphaned at the age of sixteen. The partner who looked after him was Reed McAllister. Old McAllister had enclosed a piece of literature with his last letter. It was called, "A Rift Between Friends in the War of Ideas," a pamphlet published by the Pine Tree Press

of the Freedom School, Box 165, Colorado Springs,
Colorado. This was now serving as a bookmark in the
railroad atlas.

Old McAllister generally enclosed material about
creeping socialism as opposed to free enterprise,
because, some twenty years before, Stewart had come
into his office, a wild-eyed young man, had announced
that the free enterprise system was wrong, and that he
wanted to give all his money to the poor. McAllister
had talked the rash young man out of it, but he
continued to worry about Stewart's having a relapse.
The pamphlets were prophylaxis.

McAllister needn't have bothered. Drunk or sober,
pamphlets or not, Stewart was irrevocably committed
to free enterprise now. He did not require the bucking
up in "A Rift Between Friends in the War of Ideas,"
which was supposedly a letter from a conservative to
close friends who were socialists without knowing it.
Because he did not need to, Stewart had not read what
the pamphlet had to say about the recipients of social
security and other forms of welfare, which was this:

Have we really helped these people? Look at
them well. Consider this specimen who is the end
result of our pity! What can we say to this third
generation of people to whom welfare has long
since become a way of life? Observe carefully our
handiwork whom we have spawned and are
spawning by the millions, even in times of plenty!

They do not work and will not. Heads down,
unmindful, they have neither pride nor self-respect.
They are totally unreliable, not maliciously so,
but like cattle who wander aimlessly. Foresight
and the ability to reason have simply atrophied
from long neglect. Talk to them, listen to them,
work with them as I do and you realize with a
a kind of dull horror that they have lost all
semblance of human beings except that they stand

on two feet and talk—like parrots. 'More. Give
me more. I need more,' are the only new thoughts
they have learned. . . .

They stand today as a monumental caricature of
Homo sapiens, the harsh and horrible reality
created by us out of our own misguided pity.
They are also, if we continue our present course,
the living prophecy of what a great percentage of
the rest of us will become.

And so on.

These sentiments were coals to Newcastle as far as
Stewart Buntline was concerned. He was through with
misguided pity. He was through with sex, too. And, if
the truth be told, he was fed to the teeth with the Civil
War.

R

The conversation with McAllister that had set Stewart
on the path of conservatism twenty years before was
this:

"So you want to be a saint, do you, young man?"

"I didn't say that, and I hope I didn't imply it. You
are in charge of what I inherited, money I did nothing
to earn?"

"I'll answer the first part of your question: Yes, we
are in charge of what you inherited. In reply to the
second part: If you haven't earned it yet, you will, you
shall. You come from a family that is congenitally
unable to fail to earn its way and then some. You'll lead,
my boy, because you were born to lead, and that can be
hell."

"That may or may not be, Mr. McAllister. We'll have
to wait and see about that. What I'm telling you now
is: This world is full of suffering, and money can do a
lot to relieve that suffering, and I have far more money
than I can use. I want to buy decent food and clothing
and housing for the poor, and right away."

"And, after you've done that, what would you like to be called, 'St. Stewart' or 'St. Buntline'?"

"I didn't come here to be made fun of."

"And your father didn't name us your guardians in his will because he thought we would agree politely with anything you might say. If I strike you as impudent and irreverent on the subject of would-be saints, it's because I've been through this same silly argument with so many young people before. One of the principal activities of this firm is the prevention of saintliness on the part of our clients. You think you're unusual? You're not.

"Every year at least one young man whose affairs we manage comes into our office, wants to give his money away. He has completed his first year at some great university. It has been an eventful year! He has learned of unbelievable suffering around the world. He has learned of the great crimes that are at the roots of so many family fortunes. He has had his Christian nose rubbed, often for the very first time, in the Sermon on the Mount.

"He is confused, tearful, angry! He demands to know, in hollow tones, how much money he is worth. We tell him. He goes haggard with shame, even if his fortune is based on something as honest and useful as Scotch Tape, aspirin, rugged pants for the working man, or, as in your case, brooms. You have, if I'm not mistaken, just completed one year at Harvard?"

"Yes."

"It's a great institution, but when I see the effect it has on certain young people, I ask myself, 'How dare a university teach compassion without teaching history, too?' History tells us this, my dear young Mr. Buntline, if it tells us nothing else: Giving away a fortune is a futile and destructive thing. It makes whiners of the poor, without making them rich or even comfortable. And the donor and his descendents become undistinguished members of the whining poor."

R

"A personal fortune as great as yours, Mr. Buntline,"
old McAllister went on, those many fateful years ago,
"is a miracle, thrilling and rare. You have come by it
effortlessly, and so have little opportunity to learn what
it is. In order to help you learn something about its
miraculousness, I have to offer what is perhaps an
insult. Here it is, like it or not: Your fortune is the most
important single determinant of what you think of
yourself and of what others think of you. Because of
the money, you are extraordinary. Without it, for
example, you would not now be taking the priceless
time of a senior partner in McAllister, Robjent, Reed
and McGee.

"If you give away your money, you will become
utterly ordinary, unless you happen to be a genius. You
aren't a genius, are you, Mr. Buntline?"

"No."

"Uum. And, genius or not, without money you'll
surely be less comfortable and free. Not only that, but
you will be volunteering your descendants for the muggy,
sorehead way of life peculiar to persons who might have
been rich and free, had not a soft-headed ancestor
piddled a fortune away.

"Cling to your miracle, Mr. Buntline. Money is
dehydrated Utopia. This is a dog's life for almost
everybody, as your professors have taken such pains to
point out. But, because of your miracle, life for you
and yours can be a paradise! Let me see you smile! Let
me see that you already understand what they do not
teach at Harvard until the junior year: That to be born
rich and to stay rich is something less than a felony."

R

Lila, Stewart's daughter, now went upstairs to her

bedroom. The color scheme, selected by her mother, was pink and frost. Her casement windows looked out on the harbor, on the nodding Pisquontuit Yacht Club fleet.

A forty-foot workboat named *Mary* was chugging her graceless, smoky way through the fleet, rocking the playthings. The playthings had names like *Scomber* and *Skat* and *Rosebud II* and *Follow Me* and *Red Dog* and *Bunty*. *Rosebud II* belonged to Fred and Caroline Rosewater. *Bunty* belonged to Stewart and Amanita Buntline.

Mary belonged to Harry Pena, the trap fisherman. She was a gray, lapstreak tub whose purpose was to wallow home in all weather with tons of fresh fish on board. There wasn't any shelter on her, except for a wooden box to keep the big new Chrysler dry. The wheel and the throttle and the clutch were mounted on the box. All the rest of the *Mary* was a bare-boned tub.

Harry was on his way to his traps. His two big sons, Manny and Kenny, lay head-to-head in the bow, murmuring in lazy lechery. Each boy had a six-foot tuna gaff beside him. Harry was armed with a twelve-pound mall. All three wore rubber aprons and boots. When they got to work, they would bathe in gore.

"Stop talking about fucking," said Harry. "Think about fish."

"We will, old man, when we're as old as you." This was a deeply affectionate reply.

R

An airplane came over very low, making its approach to Providence Airport. On board, reading *The Conscience of a Conservative*, was Norman Mushari.

R

The world's largest private collection of harpoons was

displayed in a restaurant called *The Weir,* which was
five miles outside of Pisquontuit. The marvellous
collection belonged to a tall homosexual from New
Bedford named Bunny Weeks. Until Bunny came down
from New Bedford and opened his restaurant,
Pisquontuit had nothing to do with whaling—ever.

Bunny called his place *The Weir* because its
Thermopane windows on the south looked out at the
fish traps of Harry Pena. There were opera glasses on
each table, in order that guests might watch Harry and
his boys clean out their traps. And when the fisherfolk
were performing out there on the briny deep, Bunny
went from table to table, explaining with gusto and
expertise what they were doing, and why. While
disserting, he would paw women shamelessly, would
never touch a man.

If guests wished to participate even more vibrantly
in the fishing business, they might order a *Horse
Mackerel Cocktail,* which was rum, grenadine, and
cranberry juice, or a *Fisherman's Salad,* which was a
peeled banana thrust through a pineapple ring, set in a
nest of chilled, creamed tuna and curly coconut shreds.

Harry Pena and his boys knew about the salad and
the cocktail and the opera glasses, though they had
never visited *The Weir.* Sometimes they would respond
to their involuntary involvement with the restaurant by
urinating off the boat. They called this ". . . *making
cream of leek soup for Bunny Weeks.*"

R

Bunny Weeks' harpoon collection lay across the rude
rafters of the gift shop that constituted the opulently
mouldy entrance to *The Weir.* The shop itself was called
The Jolly Whaler. There was a dusty skylight over the
shop, the dusty effect having been achieved by spraying
on *Jet-Spray Bon Ami,* and never wiping it off. The lattice
of rafters and harpoons underneath the skylight was

projected onto the merchandise below. The effect that Bunny had created was that real whalers, smelling of blubber and rum and sweat and ambergris, had stored their equipment in his loft. They would be coming back for it at any time.

It was through the criss-crossed shadows of harpoons that Amanita Buntline and Caroline Rosewater now shuffled. Amanita led the way, set the tone, examined the stock greedily, barbarously. As for the nature of the stock: it was everything a cold bitch might demand of an impotent husband upon rising from a scalding bath.

Caroline's manner was a wispy echo of Amanita's. Caroline was made clumsy by the fact that Amanita was forever between her and whatever seemed worth examining. The moment Amanita stopped looking at something, moved from between it and Caroline, the object somehow stopped being worth examining. Caroline was made clumsy by other facts, too, of course—that her husband worked, that she was wearing a dress that everybody knew had been Amanita's, that she had very little money in her purse.

Caroline now heard her own voice saying, as though from afar, "He certainly has good taste."

"They all do," said Amanita. "I'd rather go shopping with one than with a woman. Present company excepted, of course."

"What is it that makes them so artistic?"

"They're more sensitive, dear. They're like *us*. They *feel*."

"Oh."

R

Bunny Weeks now loped into *The Jolly Whaler*, his Topsiders squeaking as they squeegeed. He was a slender man in his early thirties. He had eyes that were standard equipment for rich American fairies—junk jewelry eyes, synthetic star sapphires with winking

Christmas-tree lights behind them. Bunny was the great grandson of the famous Captain Hannibal Weeks of New Bedford, the man who finally killed Moby Dick. No less than seven of the irons resting on the rafters overhead were said to have come from the hide of the Great White Whale.

"Amanita! Amanita!" Bunny cried fondly. He threw his arms around her, hugged her hard. "How's my girl?"

Amanita laughed.

"Something's funny?"

"Not to *me*."

"I've been hoping you'd come in today. I have a little intelligence test for you." He wanted to show her a new piece of merchandise, have her guess what it was. He hadn't greeted Caroline yet, was now obliged to do so, for she was standing between him and where he thought the object he wanted was. "Excuse me."

"I beg your pardon." Caroline Rosewater stepped aside. Bunny never seemed to remember her name, though she had been in *The Weir* at least fifty times.

Bunny failed to find what he was looking for, wheeled to search elsewhere, again found Caroline in his way. "Excuse me."

"Excuse *me*." Caroline, in getting out of his way, tripped on a cunning little milking stool, went down with one knee on the stool and both hands grasping a post.

"Oh my God!" said Bunny, annoyed with her. "Are you all right? Here! Here!" He hoisted her up, and did it in such a way that her feet kept slipping out from under her, as though she were wearing roller skates for the first time. "Are you hurt?"

Caroline smiled sloppily. "Just my dignity is all."

"Oh, the hell with your dignity, dear," he said, and he cast himself very strong as another woman when he said it. "How are your *bones*? How are your little *insides*?"

"Fine—thank you."

Bunny turned his back on her, resumed his search.

"You remember Caroline Rosewater, of course," said Amanita. It was a cruelly unnecessary thing to ask.

"Of course I remember Mrs. Rosewater," said Bunny. "Any relation to the Senator?"

"You always ask me that."

"Do I? And what do you always reply?"

"I think so—somehow—way far back—I'm almost sure."

"How interesting. He's resigning, you know."

"He is?"

Bunny faced her again. He now had a box in his hands. "Didn't he *tell* you he was going to resign?"

"No—he—"

"You don't *communicate* with him?"

"No," said Caroline bleakly, her chin pulled in.

"I'd think he'd be a very fascinating man to *communicate* with."

Caroline nodded. "Yes."

"But you don't communicate."

"No."

R

"Now then, my dear—" said Bunny, placing himself before Amanita and opening the box, "here is your intelligence test." He took from the box, which was marked "Product of Mexico," a large tin can with one end removed. The can was covered with gay wallpaper both inside and out. Glued to the unopened end was a round lace doily, and glued to the doily was an artificial water lily. "I defy you to tell me what this is for. If you tell me, and this is a seventeen-dollar item, I will give it to you free, grotesquely rich though I know you are."

"Can *I* guess, too?" said Caroline.

Bunny closed his eyes. "Of course," he whispered tiredly.

Amanita gave up at once, announcing proudly that she was dumb, that she despised tests. Caroline was about to make a chirping, bright-eyed, birdy guess, but Bunny didn't give her a chance.

"It's a cover for a spare roll of toilet paper!" said Bunny.

"That's what I was *going* to guess," said Caroline.

"Were you now?" said Bunny apathetically.

"She's a *Phi Beta Kappa*," said Amanita.

"Are you now?" said Bunny.

"Yes," said Caroline. "I don't talk about it much. I don't think about it much."

"Nor do I," said Bunny.

"You're a *Phi Beta Kappa*, too?"

"Do you mind?"

"No."

"As clubs go," said Bunny, "I've found it's a rather big one."

"Um."

"Do you like this thing, little genius?" Amanita asked Caroline, speaking of the toilet paper cover.

"Yes—it's—it's very pretty. It's sweet."

"Do you want it?"

"For seventeen *dollars?*" said Caroline. "It *is* darling." She became mournful about being poor. "Some day, maybe. Some day."

"Why not today?" asked Amanita.

"You know why not today." Caroline blushed.

"What if I were to buy it for you?"

"You mustn't! Seventeen dollars!"

"If you don't stop worrying about money so much, little bird, I'm going to have to find some other friend."

"What can I *say?*"

"Wrap it as a gift, please, Bunny."

"Oh, Amanita, thank you so much," said Caroline.

"It's no more than you deserve."

"Thank you."

"People get what they deserve," said Amanita. "Isn't that right, Bunny?"

"That's the First Law of Life," said Bunny Weeks.

R

The work boat called the *Mary* now reached the traps she served, came into view for the many drinkers and diners in the restaurant of Bunny Weeks.

"Drop your cocks and grab your socks," Harry Pena called to his snoozing sons.

He killed the engine. The momentum of the *Mary* carried her through the gate of a trap, into a ring of long poles festooned with net.

"Smell 'em?" he said. He was asking if his sons smelled all the big fish in the net.

The sons sniffed, said they did.

The big belly of the net, which might or might not hold fish, lay on the bottom. The rim of the net was in air, running from pole-tip to pole-tip in lank parabolas. The rim dipped under water at only one point. That point was the gate. It was also the mouth that would feed fish, if any, into the big belly of the net.

Now Harry himself was inside the trap. He untied a line from a cleat by the gate, hoisted away, lifted the mouth of the net into air, tied the line to the cleat again. There was no way out of the belly now—not for fish. For fish it was a bowl of doom.

The *Mary* rubbed herself gently against one side of the bowl. Harry and his sons, all in a row, reached into the sea with iron hands, pulled net into air, fed it back to the sea.

Hand-over-hand, the three were making smaller, ever smaller, the place where fish could be. And, as that place grew ever smaller, the *Mary* crept sideways across the surface of the bowl.

No one spoke. It was a magic time. Even the gulls

fell silent as the three, purified of all thought, hauled net from the sea.

R

The only place where the fish could be became an oval pool. A seeming shower of dimes flashed in the depths, and that was all. The men kept working, hand-over-hand.

The only place where the fish could be now became a curving trough, a deep one, alongside the *Mary*. It now became a shallower trough as the three men continued to work, hand-over-hand. The father and the two sons paused. A goosefish, a prehistoric monstrosity, a ten-pound tadpole studded with chancres and warts, came to the surface, opened its needle-filled mouth, surrendered. And around the goosefish, the brainless, inedible horror of cartilage, the surface of the sea was blooming with dimpled humps. Big animals were in the dark below.

Harry and his two big sons set to work again, hand-over-hand, pulling in net and feeding it back. There was almost nowhere for the fish to be. Paradoxically, the surface of the sea became mirror-like.

And then the fin of a tuna slit the mirror, was gone again.

R

In the fish trap moments later there was joyful, bloody hell. Eight big tuna were making the water heave, boil, split and roll. They shot past the *Mary*, were turned by the net, shot past again.

Harry's boys grabbed their gaffs. The younger boy thrust his hook underwater, jerked the hook into the belly of a fish, stopped the fish, turned it on a point of pure agony.

The fish came drifting alongside, languid with shock,

avoiding any motion that might make the agony worse.

Harry's younger boy gave the hook a wrenching yank. The new, deeper agony made the fish walk on his tail, topple into the *Mary* with a rubbery crash.

Harry slammed the head of the fish with his mighty mall. The fish lay still.

And another fish came crashing in. Harry slammed it on the head, too—and slammed another and another, until eight great fish lay dead.

Harry laughed, wiped his nose on his sleeve. "Son of a bitch, boys! Son of a bitch!"

The boys laughed back. All three were as satisfied with life as man can ever be.

The youngest boy thumbed his nose at the fairy's restaurant.

"Fuck 'em all, boys. Right?" said Harry.

R

Bunny came to Amanita's and Caroline's table, jingled his slave bracelet, put his hand on Amanita's shoulder, remained standing. Caroline took the opera glasses from her eyes, said a depressing thing. "It's so much like life. Harry Pena is so much like God."

"Like God?" Bunny was amused.

"You don't see what I mean?"

"I'm sure the fish do. I don't happen to be a fish. I'll tell you what I *am*, though."

"Please—not while we're eating," said Amanita.

Bunny gave a crippled little chuckle, went on with his thought. "I *am* director of a bank."

"What's that got to do with anything?" Amanita inquired.

"You find out who's broke and who isn't. And, if that's God out there, I hate to tell you, but God is bankrupt."

Amanita and Caroline expressed, each in her own

way, disbelief that a man that virile could ever have a
business failure. While they were twittering in this wise,
Bunny's hand tightened on Amanita's shoulder to the
point where she complained. "You're hurting me."

"Sorry. Didn't know it was possible."

"Bastard."

"Might as well be." And the hand bit hard again.
"That's all over," he said, meaning Harry and his sons.
The pulsing pressure of his hand let Amanita know that
he wanted very much for her to keep her mouth shut
for a change, that he was being serious for a change.
"Real people don't make their livings that way any
more. Those three romantics out there make as much
sense as Marie Antoinette and her milkmaids. When
the bankruptcy proceedings begin—in a week, a month,
a year—they'll find out that their only economic value
was as animated wallpaper for my restaurant here."
Bunny, to his credit, was not happy about this. "That's
all over, men working with their hands and backs.
They are not needed."

"Men like Harry will always win, won't they?" said
Caroline.

"They're losing everywhere." Bunny let go of
Amanita. He looked around his restaurant, invited
Amanita to do so, too, to help him count the house.
He invited them, moreover, to despise his customers
as much as he did. Almost all were inheritors. Almost
all were beneficiaries of boodles and laws that had
nothing to do with wisdom or work.

Four stupid, silly, fat widows in furs laughed over a
bathroom joke on a paper cocktail napkin.

"And look who's winning. And look who's won."

11.

NORMAN MUSHARI rented a red convertible at the
Providence Airport, drove eighteen miles to Pisquontuit
to find Fred Rosewater. As far as Mushari's employers
knew, he was in his apartment in Washington, sick in
bed. On the contrary, he felt very good.

He didn't find Fred all afternoon, for the not very
simple reason that Fred was asleep on his sailboat, a
secret thing Fred often did on warm days. There was
never much doing in life insurance for poor people on
warm afternoons.

Fred would row out to his mooring in a little yacht
club dinghy, *scree-scraw, scree-scraw,* with three inches
of freeboard all around. And he would transfer his
bulk to Rosebud II, and lie down in the cockpit, out
of sight, with his head on an orange lifejacket. He
would listen to the lapping of the water, the clinking
and creaking of the rigging, put one hand on his
genitals, feel at one with God, go to sleepy-bye. That
much was lovely.

R

The Buntlines had a young upstairs maid named Selena
Deal, who knew Fred's secret. One little window

in her bedroom looked out on the fleet. When she sat on her narrow bed and wrote, as she was doing now, her window framed the Rosebud II. Her door was ajar, so she could hear the telephone ring. That was all she had to do during the afternoons, usually—answer the telephone in case it rang. It seldom rang, and, as Selena asked herself, "Why would it?"

She was eighteen years old. She was an orphan from an orphanage that had been founded by the Buntline family in Pawtucket in 1878. When it was founded, the Buntlines required three things: That all orphans be raised as Christians, regardless of race, color, or creed, that they take an oath once a week before Sunday supper, and that, each year, an intelligent, clean female orphan enter domestic service in a Buntline home,

> . . . in order to learn about the better things in
> life, and perhaps to be inspired to climb a few
> rungs of the ladder of culture and social grace.

The oath, which Selena had taken six hundred times, before six hundred very plain suppers, went like this, and was written by Castor Buntline, poor old Stewart's great-grandfather:

> I do solemnly swear that I will respect the
> sacred private property of others, and that I will
> be content with whatever station in life God
> Almighty may assign me to. I will be grateful to
> those who employ me, and will never complain
> about wages and hours, but will ask myself
> instead, "What more can I do for my employer,
> my republic, and my God?" I understand that
> I have not been placed on Earth to be happy.
> I am here to be tested. If I am to pass the test,
> I must be always unselfish, always sober, always
> truthful, always chaste in mind, body, and deed,

and always respectful to those to whom God has,
in His Wisdom, placed above me. If I pass the
test, I will go to joy everlasting in Heaven when
I die. If I fail, I shall roast in hell while the Devil
laughs and Jesus weeps.

R

Selena, a pretty girl who played the piano beautifully
and wanted to be a nurse, was writing to the head of
the orphanage, a man named Wilfred Parrot. Parrot
was sixty. He had done a lot of interesting things in
his life, such as fighting in Spain in the Abraham
Lincoln Brigade and, from 1933 until 1936, writing
a radio serial called "Beyond the Blue Horizon." He
ran a happy orphanage. All of the children called him
"Daddy," and all of the children could cook and dance
and play some musical instrument and paint.

Selena had been with the Buntlines a month. She was
supposed to stay a year. This is what she wrote:

Dear Daddy Parrot: Maybe things will get
better here, but I don't see how. Mrs. Buntline
and I don't get along very well. She keeps saying
I am ungrateful and impertinent. I don't mean
to be, but I guess maybe I am. I just hope she
doesn't get so mad at me she turns against the
orphanage. That is the big thing I worry about. I
am just going to have to try harder to obey the
oath. What goes wrong all the time is things she
sees in my eyes. I can't keep those things out of my
eyes. She says something or does something I think
is kind of dumb or pitiful or something, and I
don't say anything about it, but she looks in my
eyes and gets very mad. One time she told me
that music was the most important thing in her
life, next to her husband and her daughter. They
have loudspeakers all over the house, all connected

to a big phonograph in the front coat closet.
There is music all day long, and Mrs. Buntline
said what she enjoyed more than anything was
picking out a musical program at the start of every
day, and loading it into the record changer. This
morning there was music coming out of all the
loudspeakers, and it didn't sound like any music
I had ever heard before. It was very high and
fast and twittery, and Mrs. Buntline was humming
along with it, rocking her head from side to side
to show me how much she loved it. It was driving
me crazy. And then her best friend, a woman
named Mrs. Rosewater, came over, and she said
how much she loved the music, too. She said
someday, when her ship came in, she would have
beautiful music all the time, too. I finally broke
down and asked Mrs. Buntline what on earth it
it was. "Why, my dear child," she said, "that is
none other than the immortal Beethoven."
"Beethoven!" I said. "Have you ever heard of him
before?" she said. "Yes, mam, I have. Daddy
Parrot played Beethoven all the time back at the
orphanage, but it didn't sound like that." So she
took me in where the phonograph was, and she
said, "Very well, I will prove it is Beethoven. I
have loaded the changer with nothing but
Beethoven. Every so often I just go on a Beethoven
binge." "I just adore Beethoven, too," Mrs.
Rosewater said. Mrs. Buntline told me to look
at what was in the record changer and tell her
whether it was Beethoven or not. It was. She
had loaded the changer with all nine symphonies,
but that poor woman had them playing at 78
revolutions per minute instead of 33, and she
couldn't tell the difference. I told her about it,
Daddy. I had to tell her, didn't I? I was very
polite, but I must have gotten that look in my
eyes, because she got very mad, and she made

me go out and clean up the chauffeur's lavatory
in the back of the garage. Actually, it wasn't a
very dirty job. They haven't had a chauffeur for
years.

R

Another time, Daddy, she took me out to watch
a sailboat race in Mr. Buntline's big motorboat.
I asked to go. I said all anybody ever seemed to
talk about in Pisquontuit was sailboat races. I
said I would like to see what was so wonderful
about them. Her daughter Lila was racing that
day. Lila is the best sailer in town. You should
see all the cups she has won. They are the main
decorations of the house. There aren't any pictures
to speak of. A neighbor has a Picasso, but I
heard him say he would a lot rather have a
daughter who could sail like Lila. I don't think it
makes much difference one way or another, but
I didn't say so. Believe me, Daddy, I don't say
half the things I could. Anyway, we went out to
see this sailboat race, and I wish you could have
heard the way Mrs. Buntline yelled and swore.
You remember the things Arthur Gonsalves used
to say? Mrs. Buntline used words that would have
been news to Arthur. I never saw a woman get so
excited and mad. She just forgot I was
there. She looked like a witch with the rabies.
You would have thought the fate of the universe
was being decided by those sunburned children in
those pretty little white boats. She finally
remembered me, and she realized she had said
some things that didn't sound very good. "You've
got to understand why we're all so excited right
now," she said. "Lila has two legs on the
Commodore's Cup." "Oh," I said, "that explains
everything." I swear, Daddy, that's all I said, but

there must have been that look in my eyes.

What gets me most about these people, Daddy, isn't how ignorant they are, or how much they drink. It's the way they have of thinking that everything nice in the world is a gift to the poor people from them or their ancestors. The first afternoon I was here, Mrs. Buntline made me come out on the back porch and look at the sunset. So I did, and I said I liked it very much, but she kept waiting for me to say something else. I couldn't think of what else I was supposed to say, so I said what seemed like a dumb thing. "Thank you very much," I said. That was exactly what she was waiting for. "You're entirely welcome," she said. I have since thanked her for the ocean, the moon, the stars in the sky, and the United States Constitution.

' Maybe I am just too wicked and dumb to realize how wonderful Pisquontuit really is. Maybe this is a case of pearls before swine, but I don't see how. I am homesick. Write soon. I love you.

Selena

P.S. Who really does run this crazy country? These creeps sure don't.

Norman Mushari killed the afternoon by driving over to Newport, paid a quarter to tour the famous Rumfoord Mansion. The queer thing about the tour was that the Rumfoords were still living there, and glaring at all comers. Moreover, they didn't need the money, God knows.

Mushari was sufficiently offended by the way that Lance Rumfoord, who was six feet eight inches tall, sneered whinnyingly at him, that he complained about it to a family servant who was guiding the tour. "If they hate the public so much," said Mushari, "they shouldn't invite them in and take their money."

This failed to gain the sympathy of the servant, who explained with acrid fatalism that the estate was open to the public for only one day out of every five years. This was required by a will now three generations old.

"Why would a will say that?"

"It was the feeling of the founder of this estate that it would be in the best interests of those living within these walls to periodically take a sampling of the sorts of people who were appearing at random outside of them." He looked Mushari up and down. "You might call it keeping up with current events. You know?"

As Mushari was leaving the estate, Lance Rumfoord came loping after him. Predatorily genial, he towered over little Mushari, explained that his mother considered herself a great judge of character, and had made the guess that Mushari had once served in the United States Infantry.

"No."

"Really? She so seldom misses. She said specifically that you had been a sniper."

"No."

Lance shrugged. "If not in this life, in some other one, then." And he sneered and whinnied again.

R

Sons of suicides often think of killing themselves at the end of a day, when their blood sugar is low. And so it was with Fred Rosewater when he came home from work. He nearly fell over the Electrolux in the living room archway, caught his balance with a quick stride, barked his shin on a little table, knocked the mints on the table to the floor. He got down on his hands and knees and picked them up.

He knew his wife was home, for the record-player Amanita had given to her for her birthday was going. She only owned five records, and they were all in the changer. They were her bonus for joining a record

club. She had gone through hell, selecting five free
records from a list of one hundred. The five she finally
chose were *Come Dance With Me,* by Frank Sinatra,
*A Mighty Fortress Is Our God, and Other Sacred
Selections,* by the Mormon Tabernacle Choir; *It's a
Long Way to Tipperary and Others,* by the Soviet Army
Chorus and Band, *The New World Symphony,*
conducted by Leonard Bernstein, and *Poems of Dylan
Thomas,* read by Richard Burton.

The Burton record was playing as Fred picked up
the mints.

Fred stood up, swayed. There were bells in his ears.
There were spots before his eyes. He went into the
bedroom, found his wife asleep in bed with her clothes
on. She was drunk, and full of chicken and mayonnaise,
as she always was after a luncheon with Amanita.
Fred tiptoed out again, thought of hanging himself
from a pipe in the cellar.

But then he remembered his son. He heard a toilet
flush, so that was where little Franklin was, in the
bathroom. He went into Franklin's bedroom to wait
for him. It was the only room in the house where
Fred felt really comfortable. The shades were drawn,
which was mildly puzzling, since there was no reason
for the boy to exclude the last of the daylight, and
there were no neighbors to peep in.

The only light came from a curious lamp on the
bedside table. The lamp consisted of a plaster statuette
of a blacksmith who had his hammer raised. There
was a pane of frosted orange glass behind the
blacksmith. And behind the glass was an electric bulb,
and over the bulb was a little tin windmill. Hot air
rising from the bulb caused the windmill to turn.
The bright surfaces of the turning mill made the light
playing on the orange glass flicker, made it look a lot
like real fire.

There was a story that went with the lamp. It was
thirty-three years old. The company that made the

lamps had been Fred's father's very last speculation.

R

Fred thought of taking a lot of sleeping pills,
remembered his son again. He looked about the weirdly
illuminated room for something to talk to the boy
about, saw the corner of the photograph sticking out
from under the pillow on the bed. Fred pulled it into
the open, thinking it was probably a picture of some
sports hero, or maybe a picture of Fred himself at
the helm of the *Rosebud II*.

But it turned out to be a pornographic picture that
little Franklin had bought that morning from Lila
Buntline, using money he earned himself on his paper
route. It showed two fat, simpering, naked whores, one
of whom was attempting to have impossible sexual
congress with a dignified, decent, unsmiling Shetland
pony.

R

Sickened, confused, Fred put the picture into his
pocket, stumbled out into the kitchen, wondered what,
in God's name, to say.

About the kitchen: an electric chair would not have
seemed out of place in it. It was Caroline's idea of a
place of torment. There was a philodendron. It had
died of thirst. In the soapdish on the sink was a mottled
ball of soap made out of many moistened slivers pressed
together. Making soap balls out of slivers was the only
household art Caroline had brought to marriage. It
was a thing her mother had taught her to do.

Fred thought of filling the bathtub with hot water,
of climbing in and slashing his wrists with a stainless
steel razorblade. But then he saw that the little plastic
garbage can in the corner was full, knew how hysterical
Caroline became if she got up from a drunken sleep

and found that no one had carried out the garbage. So
he carried it to the garage and dumped it, then washed
out the can with the hose at the side of the house.

"Frusha-frusha-blacka-blacka-burl," said the water in
the can. And Fred saw that someone had left the light
on in the cellar. He looked down through the dusty
window in an areaway, saw the top of the jelly cupboard.
Resting on it was the family history his father had
written—a history that Fred had never wished to read.
There was also a can of rat poison there, and a
thirty-eight-calibre revolver sick with rust.

It was an interesting still life. And then Fred perceived
that it wasn't entirely at rest. A little mouse was nibbling
at one corner of the manuscript.

Fred tapped on the window. The mouse hesitated,
looked everywhere but at Fred, went on nibbling
again.

Fred went down into the basement, took the
manuscript from its shelf to see how badly damaged it
was. He blew the dust from the title page, which said,
*A History of the Rosewaters of Rhode Island, by Merrihue
Rosewater*. Fred untied the string that held the
manuscript together, turned to page one, which said:

> The Old World home of the Rosewaters was
> and is in the Scilly Islands, off Cornwall. The
> founder of the family there, whose name was
> John, arrived on St. Mary Island in 1645, with
> the party accompanying the fifteen-year-old
> Prince Charles, later to become Charles the
> Second, who was fleeing the Puritan Revolution.
> The name Rosewater was then a pseudonym. Until
> John chose it for himself, there were no
> Rosewaters in England. His real name was John
> Graham. He was the youngest of the five sons of
> James Graham, Fifth Earl and First Marquis of
> Montrose. There was need for a pseudonym, for
> James Graham was a leader of the Royalist cause,

and the Royalist cause was lost. James, among
other romantic exploits, once disguised himself,
went to the Scotch Highlands, organized a small,
fierce army, and led it to six bloody victories over
the far greater forces of the Lowland Presbyterian
Army of Archibald Campbell, the Eighth Earl of
of Argyll. James was also a poet. So every
Rosewater is in fact a Graham, and has the blood
of Scotch nobility in him. James was hanged in
1650.

Poor old Fred simply could not believe this, that
he should have connection with anyone so glorious. As
it happened, he was wearing Argyll socks, and he
hitched up his trousers some to look at them. *Argyll*
had a new meaning for him now. One of his ancestors,
he told himself, had whipped the Earl of Argyll six
times. Fred noticed, too, that he had banged his shins
on a table more severely than he'd thought, for there
was blood running down to the tops of his Argylls.
He read on:

John Graham, rechristened John Rosewater in
the Scilly Island, apparently found the mild climate
and the new name congenial, for he remained
there for the rest of his life, fathering seven sons
and six daughters. He, too, is said to have been
a poet, though none of his work survives. If we
had some of his poems, they might explain to us
what must remain a mystery, why a nobleman
would give up his good name and all the privileges
it could mean, and be content to live as a simple
farmer on an island far from the centers of
wealth and power. I can make a guess, and it
can never be more than a guess, that he was
perhaps sickened by all the bloody things he saw
when he fought at his brother's side. At any rate,

he made no effort to tell his family where he was,
nor to reveal himself as Graham when royalty was
restored. In the history of the Grahams, he is said
to have been lost at sea while guarding Prince
Charles.

Fred heard Caroline throwing up now upstairs.

John Rosewater's third son, Frederick, was the
direct ancestor of the Rhode Island Rosewaters.
We know little else about him, except that he
had a son named George, who was the first
Rosewater to leave the islands. George went to
London in 1700, became a florist. George had two
sons, the younger of which, John, was imprisoned
for debt in 1731. He was freed in 1732 by James
E. Oglethorpe, who paid his debts on the condition
that John accompany Oglethorpe on an expedition
to Georgia. John was to serve as chief
horticulturalist for the expedition, which planned
to plant mulberry trees and raise silk. John
Rosewater would also become the chief architect,
laying out what was to become the city of
Savannah. In 1742, John was badly wounded in
the Battle of Bloody Marsh against the Spanish.

At this point, Fred was so elated over the
resourcefulness and bravery of his own flesh and blood
in the past, that he had to tell his wife about it at
once. And he didn't think for a moment of bringing
the sacred book to his wife. It had to stay in the holy
cellar, and she had to come down to *it*.

So he stripped the bedspread away from her,
certainly the most audacious, most blatantly sexual act
of their marriage, told her his real name was Graham,
said an ancestor of his had designed Savannah, told her
she had to come down into the cellar with him.

R

She tramped blearily down the stairs after Fred, and
he pointed to the manuscript, gave her a strident
synopsis of the history of the Rhode Island Rosewaters
up to the Battle of Bloody Marsh.

"The point I'm trying to make," he said, "is—we *are*
somebody. I am *sick* and I am *tired* of pretending that
we just aren't *anybody*."

"I never pretended we weren't anybody."

"You've pretended *I* wasn't anybody." This was
daringly true, and said almost accidentally. The truth
of it stunned them both. "You know what I mean,"
said Fred. He pressed on, did so gropingly, since he was
in the unfamiliar condition of having poignant things
to say, of being by no means at the end of them.

"These phony bastards you think are so wonderful,
compared to us—compared to *me*—I'd like to see how
many ancestors they could turn up that could compare
with mine. I've always thought people were silly who
bragged about their family trees—but, by God, if
anybody wants do any comparing, I'd be glad to show
'em mine! Let's *quit* apologizing!"

"I don't know what you mean."

"Other people say, 'Hello' or 'Goodbye!' We always
say, 'Excuse me,' no matter what we're doing." He
threw up his hands. "No more apologies! So we're
poor! All right, we're poor! This is America! And
America is one place in this sorry world where people
shouldn't *have* to apologize for being poor. The question
in America should be, 'Is this guy a good citizen? Is
he honest? Does he pull his own weight?'"

Fred hoisted the manuscript in his two plump hands,
threatened poor Caroline with it. "The Rhode Island
Rosewaters have been active, creative people in the
past, and will continue to be in the future," he told her.
"Some have had money, and some have not, but, by

God, they've played their parts in history! No more apologies!"

He had won Caroline to his way of thinking. It was a simple thing for any passionate person to do. She was ga-ga with terrified respect.

"You know what it says over the door of the National Archives in Washington?"

"No," she admitted.

" 'The past is prologue!' "

"Oh."

"All right," said Fred, "now let's read this story of the Rhode Island Rosewaters together, and try to pull our marriage together with a little mutual pride and faith."

She nodded dumbly.

R

The tale of John Rosewater at the Battle of Bloody Marsh ended the second page of the manuscript. So Fred now gripped the corner of that page between his thumb and forefinger, and dramatically peeled it from wonders lying below.

The manuscript was hollow. Termites had eaten the heart out of the history. They were still there, maggotty blue-grey, eating away.

When Caroline had clumped back up the cellar stairs, tremulous with disgust, Fred calmly advised himself that the time had come to *really* die. Fred could tie a hangman's knot blindfolded, and he tied one now in clothesline. He climbed onto a stool, tied the other end to a water pipe with a two-half hitch, which he tested.

He was putting the noose over his head, when little Franklin called down the stairway that a man wanted to see him. And the man, who was Norman Mushari, came down the stairs uninvited, lugging a fat, cross-gartered, slack-jawed briefcase.

Fred moved quickly, barely escaped being caught in the embarrassing act of destroying himself.

"Yes—?" he said to Mushari.

"Mr. Rosewater—?"

"Yes—?"

"Sir—at this very moment, your Indiana relatives are swindling you and yours out of your birthright, out of millions upon millions of dollars. I am here to tell you about a relatively cheap and simple court action that will make those millions yours."

Fred fainted.

12.

TWO DAYS LATER, it was nearly time for Eliot to get on a Greyhound Bus at the Saw City Kandy Kitchen, to go to Indianapolis to meet Sylvia in the Bluebird Room. It was noon. He was still asleep. He had had one hell of a night, not only with telephone calls, but with people coming in person at all hours, more than half of them drunk. There was panic in Rosewater. No matter how often Eliot had denied it, his clients were sure he was leaving them forever.

Eliot had cleared off the top of his desk. Laid out on it were a new blue suit, a new white shirt, a new blue tie, a new pair of black nylon socks, a new pair of Jockey shorts, a new toothbrush and a bottle of Lavoris. He had used the new toothbrush once. His mouth was a bloody wreck.

Dogs barked outside. They crossed the street from the firehouse to greet a great favorite of theirs, Delbert Peach, a town drunk. They were cheering him in his efforts to stop being a human being and become a dog. "Git! Git! Git!" he cried ineffectually. "God damn, I ain't in heat."

He tumbled in through Eliot's street-level door,

slammed the door on his best friends, climbed the stairs singing. This is what he sang:

> I've got the clap, and the blueballs, too.
> The clap don't hurt, but the blueballs do.

Delbert Peach, all bristles and stink, ran out of that song halfway up the stairs, for his progress was slow. He switched to *The Star Spangled Banner,* and he was gasping and burping and humming that when he entered Eliot's office proper.

"Mr. Rosewater? Mr. Rosewater?" Eliot's head was under his blanket, and his hands, though he was sound asleep, gripped the shroud tightly. So Peach, in order to see Eliot's beloved face, had to overcome the strength of those hands. "Mr. Rosewater—are you alive? Are you all right?"

Eliot's face was contorted by the struggle for the blanket. "What? What? What?" His eyes opened wide.

"Thank the good Lord! I dreamed you was dead!"

"Not that I know of."

"I dreamed the angels had come down from the sky, and carried you up, and set you down next to Sweet Jesus Himself."

"No," said Eliot fuzzily. "Nothing like that happened."

"It'll happen sometime. And the weeping and wailing in this town, you'll hear it up there."

Eliot hoped he wouldn't hear the weeping and wailing up there, but he didn't say so.

"Even though you're not dying, Mr. Rosewater, I know you'll never come back here. You'll get up there to Indianapolis, with all the excitement and lights and beautiful buildings, and you'll get a taste of the high life again, and you'll hunger for more of it, which is only natural for anybody who's ever tasted the high life the way you have, and the next thing you know you'll be in New York, living the very highest life there is. And why shouldn't you?"

"Mr. Peach—" and Eliot rubbed his eyes, "if I were to somehow wind up in New York, and start living the highest of all possible lives again, you know what would happen to me? The minute I got near any navigable body of water, a bolt of lightning would knock me into the water, a whale would swallow me up, and the whale would swim down to the Gulf of Mexico and up the Mississippi, up the Ohio, up the Wabash, up the White, up Lost River, up Rosewater Creek. And that whale would jump from the creek into the Rosewater Inter-State Ship Canal, and it would swim down the canal to this city, and spit me out in the Parthenon. And there I'd be."

R

"Whether you're coming back or not, Mr. Rosewater, I want to make you a present of some good news to take with you."

"And what news is that, Mr. Peach?"

"As of ten minutes ago, I swore off liquor forever. That's my present to you."

R

Eliot's red telephone rang. He lunged at it, for it was the fire department's hot line. "Hello!" He folded all the fingers of his left hand, except for the middle one. The gesture was not obscene. He was readying the finger that would punch the red button, that would make the doomsday horn on top of the firehouse bawl.

"Mr. Rosewater?" It was a woman's voice, and it was so coy.

"Yes! Yes!" Eliot was hopping up and down. Where's the fire?"

"It's in my heart, Mr. Rosewater."

Eliot was enraged, and no one would have been surprised to see him so. He was famous for his hatred of skylarking where the fire department was concerned. It was the only thing he hated. He recognized the caller, who was Mary Moody, the slut whose twins he had baptized the day before. She was a suspected arsonist, a convicted shoplifter, and a five-dollar whore. Eliot blasted her for using the hot line.

"God *damn* you for calling this number! You should go to jail and rot! Stupid sons of bitches who make personal calls on a fire department line should go to hell and fry forever!" He slammed the receiver down.

A few seconds later, the black telephone rang. "This is the Rosewater Foundation," said Eliot sweetly. "How can we help you?"

"Mr. Rosewater—this is Mary Moody again." She was sobbing.

"What on earth is the trouble, dear?" He honestly didn't know. He was ready to kill whoever had made her cry.

R

A chauffeur-driven black Chrysler Imperial pulled to the curb below Eliot's two windows. The chauffeur opened the back door. His old joints giving him pain, out came Senator Lister Ames Rosewater of Indiana. He was not expected.

He went creakingly upstairs. This abject mode of progress had not been his style in times past. He had aged shockingly, wished to demonstrate that he had aged shockingly. He did what few visitors ever did, knocked on Eliot's office door, asked if it would be all right if he came in. Eliot, who was still in his fragrant war-surplus long Johns, hurried to his father, embraced him.

"Father, Father, Father—what a wonderful surprise."

"It isn't easy for me to come here."

"I hope that isn't because you think you're not welcome."

"I can't stand the sight of this mess."

"It's certainly a lot better than it was a week ago."

"It is?"

"We had a top-to-bottom house cleaning a week ago."

The Senator winced, nudged a beer can with his toe. "Not on my account, I hope. Just because I fear an outbreak of cholera is no reason you should, too." This was said quietly.

"You know Delbert Peach, I believe?"

"I know *of* him." The Senator nodded. "How do you do, Mr. Peach. I'm certainly familiar with your war record. Deserted twice, didn't you? Or was it three times?"

Peach, cowering and sullen in the presence of such a majestic person, mumbled that he had never served in the armed forces.

"It was your father, then. I apologize. It's hard to tell how old people are, if they seldom wash or shave."

Peach admitted with his silence that it probably had been his father who had deserted three times.

"I wonder if we might not be alone for a few moments," the Senator said to Eliot, "or would that run counter to your concept of how open and friendly our society should be?"

"I'm leaving," said Peach. "I know when I'm not wanted."

"I imagine you've had plenty of opportunities to learn," said the Senator.

Peach, who was shuffling out the door, turned at this insult, surprised even himself by understanding that he had been insulted. "For a man who depends on the votes of the ordinary common people, Senator, you certainly can say mean things to them."

"As a drunk, Mr. Peach, you must surely know that drunks are not allowed in polling places."

"I've voted." This was a transparent lie.

"If you have, you've probably voted for me. Most people do, even though I never flattered the people of

Indiana in my life, not even in time of war. And do you know why they vote for me? Inside of every American, I don't care how decayed, is a scrawny, twanging old futz like me, who hates crooks and weaklings even more than I do."

R

"Gee, Father—I certainly didn't expect to see *you*. What a pleasant surprise. You look wonderful."

"I feel rotten. I have rotten news for you, too. I thought I'd better deliver it in person."

Eliot frowned slightly. "When was the last time your bowels moved?"

"None of your business!"

"Sorry."

"I'm not here for a cathartic. The C.I.O. says my bowels haven't moved since the National Recovery Act was declared unconstitutional, but that's not why I'm here."

"You said everything was so *rotten*."

"So?"

"Usually, when somebody comes in here and says that, nine times out of ten, it's a case of constipation."

"I'll tell you what the news is, boy, and then let's see if *you* can cheer up with Ex-Lax. A young lawyer working for McAllister, Robjent, Reed and McGee, with full access to all the confidential files about you, has quit. He's hired out to the Rhode Island Rosewaters. They're going to get you in court. They're going to prove you're insane."

The buzzer of Eliot's alarm clock went off. Eliot picked up the clock, went to the red button on the wall. He watched the sweep secondhand of the clock intently, his lips working, counting off the seconds. He aimed the blunt middle finger of his left hand at the button, suddenly stabbed, thus activating the loudest fire alarm in the Western Hemisphere.

The awful shout of the horn hurled the Senator against a wall, curled him up with his hands over his his ears. A dog in New Ambrosia, seven miles away, ran in circles, bit his tail. A stranger in the Saw City Kandy Kitchen threw coffee all over himself and the proprietor. In Bella's Beauty Nook in the basement of the Court House, three-hundred-pound Bella had a mild heart attack. And wits throughout the county poised themselves to tell a tired and untruthful joke about Fire Chief Charley Warmergram, who had an insurance office next to the firehouse: "Must have scared Charley Warmergram half out of his secretary."

Eliot released the button. The great alarm began to swallow its own voice, speaking gutturally and interminably of *"bubblegum, bubblegum, bubblegum."*

There was no fire. It was simply high noon in Rosewater.

R

"What a racket!" the Senator mourned, straightening up slowly. "I've forgotten everything I ever knew."

"That might be nice."

"Did you hear what I said about the Rhode Island people?"

"Yes."

"And how does it make you feel?"

"Sad and frightened." Eliot sighed, tried a wistful smile, couldn't manage one. "I had hoped it would never have to be proved, that it would never matter one way or another—whether I was sane or not."

"You have some doubts as to your own sanity?"

"Certainly."

"And how long has *this* been going on?"

Eliot's eyes widened as he sought an honest answer. "Since I was ten, maybe."

R

"I'm sure you're joking."

"That's a comfort."

"You were a sturdy, sane little boy."

"I was?" Eliot was ingenuously charmed by the little boy he had been, was glad to think about him rather than about the spooks that were closing in on him.

"I'm only sorry we brought you out here."

"I loved it out here. I still do," Eliot confessed dreamily.

The Senator moved his feet slightly apart, making a firmer base for the blow he was about to deliver. "That may be, boy, but it's time to go now—and never come back."

"Never come back?" Eliot echoed marvelingly.

"This part of your life is over. It had to end sometime. I'll thank the Rhode Island vermin for this much: They're forcing you to leave, and to leave right now."

"How can they do *that?*"

"How do you expect to defend your sanity with a backdrop like this?"

Eliot looked about himself, saw nothing remarkable. "This looks—this looks—*peculiar?*"

"You know damn well it does."

Eliot shook his head slowly. "You'd be surprised what I don't know, Father."

"There's no institution like this anywhere else in the world. If this were a set on a stage, and the script called for the curtain to go up with no one on stage, when the curtain went up, the audience would be on pins and nedles, eager to see the incredible nut who could live this way."

"What if the nut came out and gave sensible explanations for his place being the way it is?"

"He would still be a nut."

R

Eliot accepted this, or seemed to. He didn't argue with
it, allowed that he had better wash up and get dressed
for his trip. He rummaged through his desk drawers,
found a small paper bag containing purchases he had
made the day before, a bar of *Dial* soap, a bottle of
Absorbine, Jr., for his athlete's foot, a bottle of *Head
and Shoulders* shampoo for his dandruff, a bottle of *Arrid*
roll-on deodorant, and a tube of *Crest* toothpaste.

"I'm glad to see you taking pride in your appearance
again, boy."

"Hm?" Eliot was reading the label on the *Arrid*,
which he had never used before. He had never used *any*
underarm deodorant before.

"You get cleaned up, and cut down on the booze, clear
out of here, open a decent office in Indianapolis or
Chicago or New York, and, when the hearing comes up,
they'll see you're as sane as anybody."

"Uum." Eliot asked his father if *he* had ever used
Arrid.

The Senator was offended. "I shower every morning
and night. I presume that takes care of any fulsome
effluvium."

"It says here that you might get a rash, and you
should stop using it, if you get a rash."

"If it worries you, don't use it. Soap and water are
the important things."

"Um."

"That's one of the troubles with this country," said
the Senator. "The Madison Avenue people have made
us all more alarmed about our own armpits than about
Russia, China and Cuba combined."

The conversation, actually a very dangerous one
between two highly vulnerable men, had drifted into a
small area of peace. They could agree with one another,
and not be afraid.

"You know—" said Eliot, "Kilgore Trout once wrote a whole book about a country that was devoted to fighting odors. That was the national purpose. There wasn't any disease, and there wasn't any crime, and there wasn't any war, so they went after odors."

"If you get in court," said the Senator, "it would be just as well if you didn't mention your enthusiasm for Trout. Your fondness for all that Buck Rogers stuff might make you look immature in the eyes of a lot of people."

The conversation had left the area of peace again. Eliot's voice was edgy as he persisted in telling the story by Trout, which was called *Oh Say Can You Smell?*

"This country," said Eliot, "had tremendous research projects devoted to fighting odors. They were supported by individual contributions given to mothers who marched on Sundays from door to door. The ideal of the research was to find a specific chemical deodorant for every odor. But then the hero, who was also the country's dictator, made a wonderful scientific breakthrough, even though he wasn't a scientist, and they didn't need the projects any more. He went right to the root of the problem."

"Uh huh," said the Senator. He couldn't stand stories by Kilgore Trout, was embarrassed for his son. "He found one chemical that would eliminate all odors?" he suggested, to hasten the tale to a conclusion.

"No. As I say, the hero was dictator, and he simply eliminated noses."

* R *

Eliot was now taking a full bath in the frightful little lavatory, shivering and barking and coughing as he sloshed himself with sopping paper towels.

His father could not watch, roamed the office instead, averting his eyes from the obscene and ineffectual ablutions. There was no lock on the office door, and

Eliot had, at his father's insistence, shoved a filing
cabinet against it. "What if somebody should walk in
here see you stark naked?" the Senator had demanded.
And Eliot had responded, "To these people around
here, Father, I'm no particular sex at all."

So the Senator pondered that unnatural sexlessness
along with all the other evidences of insanity,
disconsolately pulled open the top drawer of the filing
cabinet. There were three cans of beer in it, a 1948
New York State driver's license, and an unsealed
envelope, addressed to Sylvia in Paris, never mailed.
In the envelope was a love poem from Eliot to Sylvia,
dated two years before.

The Senator thrust aside shame and read the poem,
hoping to learn from it things that might defend his
son. This was the poem he read, and he was not able to
keep shame away when he was through:

> "I'm a painter in my dreams, you know,
>   Or maybe you didn't know. And a sculptor.
> Long time no see.
> And a kick to me
> Is the interplay of materials
> And these hands of mine.
> And some of the things I would do to you
> Might surprise you.
> For instance, if I were there with you as
>   you read this,
> And you were lying down,
> I might ask you to bare your belly
> In order that I might take my left thumbnail
> And draw a straight line five inches long
> Above your pubic hair.
> And then I might take the index finger
> Of my right hand,
> And insinuate it just over the rim of the
>   right side
> Of your famous belly button,

                And leave it there, motionless, for maybe
                    half an hour.
                Queer?
                You bet."

The Senator was shocked. It was the mention of
pubic hair that really appalled him. He had seen very
few naked bodies in his time, perhaps five or six, and
pubic hair was to him the most unmentionable,
unthinkable of all materials.

Now Eliot came out of the lavatory, all naked and
hairy, drying himself with a tea towel. The tea towel
was new. It still had a price tag on it. The Senator
was petrified, felt beset by overwhelming forces of filth
and obscenity on all sides.

Eliot did not notice. He continued to dry himself
innocently, then threw the tea towel into the wastebasket.
The black telephone rang.

"This is the Rosewater Foundation. How can we
help you?"

"Mr. Rosewater—" said a woman, "there was a thing
on the radio about you."

"Oh?" Eliot now began to play unconsciously with
his pubic hair. It was nothing extravagant. He would
simply uncoil a tight spring of it, let it snap back into
place

"It said they were going to try to prove you were
crazy."

"Don't worry about it, dear. There's many a slip
betwixt the cup and the lip."

"Oh, Mr. Rosewater—if you go away and never
come back, we'll die."

"I give you my word of honor I'm coming back. How
is that?"

"Maybe they won't *let* you come back."

"Do you think I'm crazy, dear?"

"I don't know how to put it."

"Any way you like."

"I can't help thinking people are going to *think* you're crazy for paying so much attention to people like us."

"Have you seen the other people there are to pay attention to?"

"I never been out of Rosewater County."

"It's worth a trip, dear. When I get back, why don't I give you a trip to New York?"

"Oh God! But you're never coming back!"

"I gave you my word of honor."

"I know, I know—but we all feel it in our bones, we smell it in the air. You're not coming back."

Eliot had now found a hair that was a lulu. He kept extending and extending it until it was revealed as being one foot long. He looked down at it, then glanced at his father, incredulously proud of owning such a thing.

The Senator was livid.

"We tried to plan all kinds of ways to say good-bye to you, Mr. Rosewater," the woman went on. "Parades and signs and flags and flowers. But you won't see a one of us. We're all too scared."

"Of what?"

"I don't know." She hung up.

R

Eliot pulled on his new Jockey shorts. As soon as they were snugly on, his father spoke grimly.

"Eliot—"

"Sir—?" Eliot was running his thumbs pleasurably under the elasticized belly-band. "These things certainly give support. I'd forgotten how nice it was to *have* support."

The Senator blew up. "Why do you *hate* me so?" he cried.

Eliot was flabbergasted. "Hate you? Father—I don't hate you. I don't hate anybody."

"Your every act and word is aimed at hurting me as much as you possibly can!"

"No!"

"I have no idea what I ever did to you that you're paying me back for now, but the debt must surely be settled by now."

Eliot was shattered. "Father—please—"

"Get away! You'll only hurt me more, and I can't stand any more pain."

"For the love of God—"

"Love!" the Senator echoed bitterly. "You certainly loved me, didn't you? Loved me so much you smashed up every hope or ideal I ever had. And you certainly loved Sylvia, didn't you?'

Eliot covered his ears.

The old man raved on, spraying fine beads of spit. Eliot could not hear the words, but lip-read the terrible story of how he had ruined the life and health of a woman whose only fault had been to love him.

The Senator stormed out of the office, was gone.

Eliot uncovered his ears, finished dressing, as though nothing special had happened. He sat down to tie his shoelaces. When these were tied, he straightened up. And he froze as stiff as any corpse.

The black telephone rang. He did not answer.

13.

SOMETHING THERE WAS in Eliot, though, that watched the clock. Ten minutes before his bus was due at the Saw City Kandy Kitchen, he thawed, arose, pursed his lips, picked some lint from his suit, went out his office door. He had no surface memory of the fight with his father. His step was jaunty, that of a Chaplinesque *boulevardier*.

He bent to pat the heads of dogs who welcomed him to street level. His new clothes hampered him, bound him in the crotch and armpits, crackled as though lined with newspaper, reminded him of how nicely turned out he was.

There was talk coming from the lunchroom. Eliot listened without showing himself. He did not recognize any of the voices, although they belonged to friends of his. Three men were talking ruefully of money, which they did not have. There were many pauses, for thoughts came to them almost as hard as money did.

"Well," said one at last, "it ain't no disgrace to be poor." This line was the first half of a fine old joke by the Hoosier humorist, Kin Hubbard.

"No," said another man, completing the joke, "but it might as well be."

R

Eliot crossed the street, went into Fire Chief Charley
Warmergran's insurance office. Charles was not a pitiful
person, had never applied to the Foundation for help
of any kind. He was one of about seven in the county
who had actually done quite well under real free
enterprise. Bella of Bella's Beauty Nook was another.
Both of them had started with nothing, both were
children of brakemen on the Nickel Plate. Charley was
ten years younger than Eliot. He was six-feet-four, had
broad shoulders, no hips, no belly. In addition to being
Fire Chief, he was Federal Marshal and Inspector of
Weights and Measures. He also owned, jointly with
Bella, La Boutique de Paris, which was a nice little
haberdashery and notions store in the new shopping
center for the well-to-do people in New Ambrosia.
Like all real heroes, Charley had a fatal flaw. He refused
to believe that he had gonorrhea, whereas the truth
was that he did.

R

Charley's famous secretary was on an errand. The only
other person there when Eliot walked in was Noyes
Finnerty, who was sweeping the floor. Noyes had been
the center of the immortal Noah Rosewater Memorial
High School Basketball Team which went undefeated in
1933. In 1934, Noyes strangled his sixteen-year-old wife
for notorious infidelity, went to prison for life. Now he
was paroled, thanks to Eliot. He was fifty-one. He had
no friends, no relatives. Eliot found out about his being
in prison by accident, while leafing through old copies
of *The Rosewater County Clarion Call,* made it his
business to get him paroled.

Noyes was a quiet, cynical, resentful man. He had
never thanked Eliot for anything. Eliot was neither

hurt nor startled. He was used to ingratitude. One of
his favorite Kilgore Trout books dealt with ingratitude
and nothing else. It was called, *The First District Court
of Thankyou,* which was a court you could take people
to, if you felt they hadn't been properly grateful for
something you had done. If the defendant lost his case,
the court gave him a choice between thanking the
plaintiff in public, or going into solitary confinement
on bread and water for a month. According to Trout,
eighty per cent of those convicted chose the black hole.

R

Noyes was a lot faster than Charley in perceiving that
Eliot was far from well. He stopped sweeping, watched
acutely. He was a mean voyeur. Charley, enchanted by
memories of so many fires at which he and Eliot had
behaved so well, did not become suspicious until Eliot
congratulated him on having just won an award which
he had in fact won three years before.

"Eliot—are you kidding?"

"Why would I kid you? I think it's a wonderful
honor." They were discussing the Young Hoosier
Horatio Alger Award for 1962, awarded to Charley
by the Indiana Federation of Conservative Young
Republican Businessmen's Clubs.

"Eliot—" said Charley wincingly, "that was three
years ago."

"It was?"

Charley arose from his desk. "And you and I sat up
in your office, and we decided to send the damn plaque
back."

"We did?"

"We went over the history of the thing, and we
decided it was the kiss of death."

"Why would we decide that?"

"*You* were the one who dug up the history, Eliot."
Eliot frowned ever so slightly. "I've forgotten." The

little frown was a formality. The forgetting didn't really bother him.

"They started giving the thing in 1945. They'd given it sixteen times before I won it. Don't you remember now?"

"No."

"Out of sixteen winners of the Young Hoosier Horatio Alger Award, six were behind bars for fraud or income-tax evasion, four were under indictment for one thing or another, two had falsified their war records, and one actually went to the electric chair."

R

"Eliot—" said Charley with mounting anxiety, "did you hear what I just said?"

"Yes," said Eliot.

"What did I just say?"

"I forget."

"You just said you heard me."

Noyes Finnerty spoke up. "All he hears is the big click." He came forward for a closer examination of Eliot. His approach was not sympathetic. It was clinical. Eliot's response was clinical, too, as though a nice doctor were shining a bright light in his eyes, looking for something. "He heard that *click,* man. Man, did he ever hear that *click.*"

"What the hell are you talking about?" Charley asked him.

"It's a thing you learn to listen for in prison."

"We're not in prison now."

"It ain't a thing that happens just in prison. In prison, though, you get to listening for things more and more. You stay there long enough, you go blind, you're all ears. The click is one thing you listen for. You two—you think you're mighty close? If you were really close—and that don't mean you have to like him, just *know* him—you would have heard that *click*

of his a mile away. You get to know a man, and down
deep there's something bothering him bad, and maybe
you never find out what it is, but it's what makes him
do like he does, it's what makes him look like he's got
secrets in his eyes. And you tell him, 'Calm down,
calm down, take it easy now.' Or you ask him, 'How
come you keep doing the same crazy things over and
over again, when you know they're just going to get
you in trouble again?' Only you know there's no sense
arguing with him, on account of it's the thing inside
that's making him go. It says, 'Jump,' he jumps. It says,
'Steal,' he steals. It says, 'Cry,' he cries. Unless he dies
young, though, or unless he gets everything all his
way and nothing big goes wrong, that thing inside of
him is going to run down like a wind-up toy. You're
working in the prison laundry next to this man. You've
known him twenty years. You're working along, and
all of a sudden you hear this *click* from him. You turn
to look at him. He's stopped working. He's all calmed
down. He looks real dumb. He looks real sweet.
You look in his eyes, and the secrets are gone. He can't
even tell you his own name right then. He goes back to
work, but he'll never be the same. That thing that
bothered him so will never click on again. It's dead,
it's *dead*. And that part of that man's life where he
had to be a certain crazy way, that's *done!*"

Noyes, who had begun with such a massive lack of
passion, was now rigid and perspiring. Both of his hands
were white, choking the broomhandle in a deathgrip.
And while the natural design of his story suggested that
he calm down, to illustrate how nicely the man next
to him in the laundry had calmed down, it was
impossible for him to simulate peace. The wrenching
work his hands did on the broomhandle became obscene,
and the passion that would not die made him nearly
inarticulate. "Done! Done!" he insisted. It was the
broomhandle that enraged him most now. He tried to
snap it across his thigh, snarled at Charley, the owner

of the broom, "The son of a bitch won't break! Won't break!

"You lucky bastard," he said to Eliot, still trying to break the broom, "you've had yours!" He showered Eliot with obscenities.

He flung the broom away. "Motherfucker won't break!" he cried, and he stormed out the door.

R

Eliot was unruffled by the scene. He asked Charley mildly what the man had against brooms. He said, too, that he guessed he had better catch his bus.

"Are—are you all right, Eliot?"

"I'm wonderful."

"You are?"

"I never felt better in my life. I feel as though—as though—"

"Yeah—?"

"As though some marvelous new phase of my life were about to begin."

"That must be nice."

"It is! It is!"

R

And that continued to be Eliot's mood as he sauntered to the Saw City Kandy Kitchen. The aspect of the street was unnaturally quiet, as though a gun fight were expected, but Eliot did not notice this. The town was certain he was leaving forever. Those most dependent on Eliot had heard the *click* as clearly as they would have heard a cannon shot. There had been a lot of frantic, lame-brained planning of an appropriate farewell—a firemen's parade, a demonstration with placards saying the things that most needed saying, a triumphal arch of water from fire hoses. The plans had all collapsed. There was no one to organize such a thing, to lead. Most were so eviscerated by the prospect of Eliot's leaving that they could not find the energy or bravery to stand at the rear of a large crowd, even, and feebly wave bye-bye. They knew the street down which he would walk. From that most fled.

Eliot left the afternoon dazzle of the sidewalk for the humid shade of the Parthenon, strolled along the canal. A retired saw-maker, a man about the Senator's age, was fishing with a bamboo pole. He was seated on a camp stool. A transistor radio was on the pavement between his high shoes. The radio was playing "Ol' Man River." "Darkies all work," it said, "while the white folks play."

The old man wasn't a drunk or a pervert or anything. He was simply old, and a widower, and shot full of cancer, and his son in the Strategic Air Command never wrote, and his personality wasn't much. Booze upset him. The Rosewater Foundation had given him a grant for morphine, which his doctor prescribed.

Eliot greeted him, found he could not remember his name, nor what his trouble was. Eliot filled his lungs. It was too fine a day for sad things anyway.

R

At the far end of the Parthenon, which was a tenth of a mile long, was a small stand that sold shoelaces, razorblades, soft drinks, and copies of *The American Investigator*. It was run by a man named Lincoln Ewald, who had been an ardent Nazi sympathizer during the Second World War. During that war, Ewald had set up a short-wave transmitter, in order to tell the Germans what was being produced by the Rosewater Saw Company every day, which was paratroop knives and armor plate. His first message, and the Germans hadn't asked him for any messages at all, was to the effect that, if they could bomb Rosewater, the entire American economy would shrivel and die. He didn't ask for money in exchange for the information. He sneered at money, said that that was why he hated America, because money was king. He wanted an Iron Cross, which he requested be sent in a plain wrapper.

His message was received loud and clear on the walkie-talkies of two game wardens in Turkey Run State Park, forty-two miles away. The wardens spilled the beans to the Federal Bureau of Investigation, who arrested Ewald at the address to which the Iron Cross was to be sent. He was put in a mental institution until the war was over.

The Foundation had done very little for him, except to listen to his political views, which no one else would do. The only things Eliot ever bought him were a cheap phonograph and a set of German lessons on records. Ewald wanted so much to learn German, but he was too excited and angry all the time.

Eliot couldn't remember Ewald's name, either, and nearly passed him by without seeing him. His sinister little leper's booth there in the ruin of a great civilization was easy to miss.

"Heil Hitler," said Ewald in a grackle voice.

Eliot stopped, looked amiably at the place from which the greeting had come. Ewald's booth was curtained by copies of *The American Investigator*. The curtains seemed to be polka-dotted. The polka dots were the belly-buttons of Randy Herald, the cover girl. And she asked over and over again for a man who could give her a baby that would be a genius.

"Heil Hitler," said Ewald again. He did not part the curtains.

"And Heil Hitler to you, sir," said Eliot smiling, "and good-bye."

R

The barbaric sunshine slammed Eliot as he stepped from the Parthenon. His momentarily injured eyes saw

two loafers on the courthouse steps as charred stickmen
surrounded by steam. He heard Bella, down in her
beauty nook, bawling out a woman for not taking
good care of her fingernails.

Eliot encountered no one for quite a while, although
he did catch someone peeking at him from a window.
He winked and waved to whomever it was. When he
reached Noah Rosewater Memorial High School, which
was closed tight for the summer, he paused before the
flagpole, indulged himself in shallow melancholy. He
was taken by the sounds of the hollow iron pole's
being tapped and caressed despondently by the hardware
on the empty halyard.

He wanted to comment on the sounds, to have
someone else listen to them, too. But there was nobody
around but a dog that had been following him, so he
spoke to the dog. "That's such an *American* sound, you
know? School out and the flag down? Such a sad
American sound. You should hear it sometime when
the sun's gone down, and a light evening wind comes
up, and it's suppertime all around the world."

A lump grew in his throat. It felt good.

R

As Eliot passed the Sunoco station, a young man crept
from between two pumps. He was Roland Barry, who
had suffered a nervous breakdown ten minutes after
being sworn into the Army at Fort Benjamin Harrison.
He had a one hundred per cent disability pension. His
breakdown came when he was ordered to take a
shower with one hundred other men. The pension
was no joke. Roland could not speak above a whisper.
He spent many hours a day between the pumps,
pretending to strangers that he had something to do with
something there. "Mr. Rosewater—?" he whispered.

Eliot smiled, held out his hand. "You'll have to
forgive me—I've forgotten your name."

Roland's self-esteem was so low that he was not surprised at being forgotten by a man whom he had visited at least once a day for the past year. "Wanted to thank you for saving my life."

"For what?"

"My life, Mr. Rosewater—you saved it, whatever it is."

"You're exaggerating, surely."

"You're the only one who didn't think what happened to me was funny. Maybe you won't think a poem is funny, either." He thrust a piece of paper into Eliot's hand. "I cried while I wrote it. That's how funny it was to me. That's how funny everything is to me." He ran away.

Perplexed, Eliot read the poem, which went like this:

> "Lakes, carillons,
> Pools and bells,
> Fifes and freshets,
> Harps and wells;
> Flutes and rivers,
> Streams, bassoons,
> Geysers, trumpets,
> Chimes, lagoons.
> Hear the music,
> Drink the water,
> As we poor lambs
> All go to slaughter.
> I love you Eliot.
> Good-bye. I cry.
> Tears and violins.
> Hearts and flowers,
> Flowers and tears.
> Rosewater, good-bye."

Eliot arrived at the Saw City Kandy Kitchen without further incident. Only the proprietor and one customer were inside. The customer was a fourteen-year-old nymphet, pregnant by her stepfather, which stepfather was in prison now. The Foundation was paying for her medical care. It had also reported the stepfather's crime to the police, had subsequently hired for him the best Indiana lawyer that money could buy.

The girl's name was Tawny Wainwright. When she brought her troubles to Eliot, he asked her how her spirits were. "Well," she said, "I guess I don't feel too *bad*. I guess this is as good a way as any to start out being a movie star."

She was drinking a Coca Cola and reading *The American Investigator* now. She glanced furtively at Eliot once. That was the last time.

R

"A ticket to Indianapolis, please."

"One way or round trip, Eliot?"

Eliot did not hesitate. "One way, if you please."

Tawny's glass nearly toppled. She caught it in time.

"One way to Indianapolis!" said the proprietor loudly. "Here you are, sir!" He validated Eliot's ticket with a stamp savagely, handed over the ticket, turned quickly away. He didn't look at Eliot again, either.

Eliot, unaware of any strain, drifted over to the magazine and book racks for something to read on the trip. He was tempted by the *Investigator,* opened it, scanned a story about a seven-year-old girl who had had her head eaten off by a bear in Yellowstone Park in 1934. He returned it to the rack, selected instead a paperback book by Kilgore Trout. It was called *Pan-Galactic Three-Day Pass.*

The bus blew its flatulent horns outside.

R

As Eliot boarded the bus, Diana Moon Glampers

appeared. She was sobbing. She was carrying her white
Princess telephone, dragging its uprooted wire behind
her. "Mr. Rosewater!"

"Yes?"

She smashed the telephone on the pavement by the
door of the bus. "I don't need a telephone any more.
Nobody for me to call up. Nobody to call me up."

He sympathized with her, but he did not recognize
her. "I'm—I'm sorry. I don't understand."

"You don't *what?*"

"It's *me*, Mr. Rosewater! It's Diana! It's Diana Moon
Glampers!"

"I'm pleased to meet you."

"Pleased to *meet* me?"

"I really *am*—but—but, what's this about a
telephone?"

"You were the only reason I *needed* one."

"Oh, now—" he said, doubtingly, "you surely have
many other acquaintances."

"Oh, Mr. Rosewater—" she sobbed, and she sagged
against the bus, "you're my *only* friend."

"You can make more, surely," Eliot suggested
hopefully.

"Oh God!" she cried.

"You could join some church group, perhaps."

"*You're* my church group! You're my *everything!*
You're my government. You're my husband. You're
my friends."

These claims made Eliot uncomfortable. "You're
very nice to say so. Good luck to you. I really have to
be going now." He waved. "Good-bye."

R

Eliot now began to read *Pan-Galactic Three-Day Pass*.
There was more fussing outside the bus, but Eliot
didn't think it had anything to do with him. He was
immediately enchanted by the book, so much so that he

didn't even notice when the bus pulled away. It was an exciting story, all about a man who was serving on a sort of Space-Age Lewis and Clark Expedition. The hero's name was Sergeant Raymond Boyle.

The expedition had reached what appeared to be the absolute and final rim of the Universe. There didn't seem to be anything beyond the solar system they were in, and they were setting up equipment to sense the faintest signals that might be coming from the slightest anything in all that black velvet nothing out there.

Sergeant Boyle was an Earthling. He was the only Earthling on the expedition. In fact, he was the only creature from the Milky Way. The other members were from all over the place. The expedition was a joint effort supported by about two hundred galaxies. Boyle wasn't a technician. He was an English teacher. The thing was that Earth was the only place in the whole known Universe where language was used. It was a unique Earthling invention. Everybody else used mental telepathy, so Earthlings could get pretty good jobs as language teachers just about anywhere they went.

The reason creatures wanted to use language instead of mental telepathy was that they found out they could get so much more *done* with language. Language made them so much more *active*. Mental telepathy, with everybody constantly telling everybody everything, produced a sort of generalized indifference to *all* information. But language, with its slow, narrow meanings, made it possible to think about one thing at a time—to start thinking in terms of *projects*.

Boyle was called out of his English class, was told to report at once to the commanding officer of the expedition. He couldn't imagine what it was all about. He went into the C.O.'s office, saluted the old man. Actually, the C.O. didn't look anything like an old man. He was from the planet *Tralfamadore,* and was about as tall as an Earthling beer can. Actually, he didn't look like a beer can, either. He looked like a little plumber's friend.

He wasn't alone. The chaplain of the expedition was there, too. The padre was from the planet Glinko-X-3. He was an enormous sort of Portuguese man-o'-war, in a tank of sulfuric acid on wheels. The chaplain looked grave. Something awful had happened.

The chaplain told Boyle to be brave, and then the C.O. told him there was very bad news from home. The C.O. said there had been a death back home, that Boyle was being given an emergency three-day pass, that he should get ready to leave right away.

> "Is it—is it—Mom?" said Boyle, fighting back the tears. "Is it Pop? Is it Nancy?" Nancy was the girl next door. "Is it Gramps?"
>
> "Son—" said the C.O., "brace yourself. I hate to tell you this: It isn't *who* has died. It's *what* has died."
>
> "What's died?"
>
> "What's died, my boy, is the Milky Way."

Eliot looked up from his reading. Rosewater County was gone. He did not miss it.

R

When the bus stopped in Nashville, Indiana, the seat of Brown County, Eliot glanced up again, studied the fire apparatus on view there. He thought of buying Nashville some really nice equipment, but decided against it. He didn't think the people would take good care of it.

Nashville was an arts and crafts center, so it wasn't surprising that Eliot also saw a glassblower making Christmas-tree ornaments in June.

R

Eliot didn't look up again until the bus reached the outskirts of Indianapolis. He was astonished to see that the entire city was being consumed by a fire-storm. He had never seen a fire-storm, but he had certainly read and dreamed about many of them.

He had a book hidden in his office, and it was a mystery even to Eliot as to why he should hide it, why he should feel guilty every time he got it out, why he should be afraid of being caught reading it. His feelings about the book were those of a weak-willed puritan with respect to pornography, yet no book could be more innocent of eroticism than the book he hid. It was called *The Bombing of Germany*. It was written by Hans Rumpf.

And the passage Eliot would read over and over again, his features blank, his palms sweating, was this description of the fire-storms in Dresden:

> As the many fires broke through the roofs of the burning buildings, a column of heated air rose more than two and a half miles high and one and a half miles in diameter. . . . This column was turbulent, and it was fed from its base by in-rushing cooler ground-surface air. One and one and a half miles from the fires this draught increased the wind velocity from eleven to thirty-three miles per hour. At the edge of the area the velocities must have been appreciably greater, as trees three feet in diameter were uprooted. In a short time the temperature reached ignition point for all combustibles, and the entire area was ablaze. In such fires complete burn-out occurred; that is, no trace of combustible material remained, and only after two days were the areas cool enough to approach.

Eliot, rising from his seat in the bus, beheld the fire-storm of Indianapolis. He was awed by the majesty of the column of fire, which was at least eight miles in diameter and fifty miles high. The boundaries of the column seemed absolutely sharp and unwavering, as though made of glass. Within the boundaries, helixes of dull red embers turned in stately harmony about an inner core of white. The white seemed holy.

14.

EVERYTHING WENT BLACK for Eliot, as black as what
lay beyond the ultimate rim of the universe. And then
he awoke to find himself sitting on the flat rim of a dry
fountain. He was dappled by sunlight filtering down
through a sycamore tree. A bird was singing in the
sycamore tree. *"Poo-tee-weet?"* it sang. *"Poo-tee-weet.
Weet, weet, weet."* Eliot was within a high garden wall,
and the garden was familiar. He had spoken to Sylvia
many times in just this place. It was the garden of Dr.
Brown's private mental hospital in Indianapolis, to
which he had brought her so many years before. These
words were cut into the fountain rim:

> "Pretend to be good always, and even God
> will be fooled."

Eliot found that someone had dressed him for tennis,
all in snowy white, and that, as though he were a
department store display, someone had even put a
tennis racket in his lap. He closed his hand around
the racket handle experimentally, to discover whether
it was real and whether he was real. He watched the
play of the intricate basketwork of his forearm's
musculature, sensed that he was not only a tennis

player, but a good one. And he did not wonder where
it was that he played tennis, for one side of the garden
was bounded by a tennis court, with morning-glories
and sweet peas twining in the chicken wire.

"Poo-tee-weet?"

Eliot looked up at the bird and all the green leaves,
understood that this garden in downtown Indianapolis
could not have survived the fire he saw. So there had
been no fire. He accepted this peacefully.

R

He continued to look up at the bird. He wished that
he were a dicky bird, so that he could go up into the
treetop and never come down. He wanted to fly up so
high because there was something going on at
ground-zero that did not make him feel good. Four
men in dark business suits were seated chockablock on
a concrete bench only six feet away. There were staring
at him hard, expecting something significant from him.
And it was Eliot's feeling that he had nothing of
significance to say or give.

The muscles in the back of his neck were aching
now. They couldn't hold his head tipped back forever.

"Eliot—?"

"Sir—?" And Eliot knew that he had just spoken to
his father. He now brought his gaze down from the
tree gradually, let it drop like a sick dicky bird from
twig to twig. His eyes were at last on level with those
of his father.

"You were going to tell us something important,"
his father reminded him.

Eliot saw that there were three old men and one
young one on the bench, all sympathetic, and listening
intently for whatever he might care to say. The young
man he recognized as Dr. Brown. The second old man
was Thurmond McAllister, the family lawyer. The third
old man was a stranger. Eliot could not name him,

and yet, in some way that did not disturb Eliot, the
man's features, those of a kindly country undertaker,
claimed him as a close friend, indeed.

R

"You can't find the words?" Dr. Brown suggested.
There was a tinge of anxiety in the healer's voice, and
he shifted about, putting body English on whatever
Eliot was about to do.

"I can't find the words," Eliot agreed.

"Well," said the Senator, "if you can't put it into
words, you certainly can't use it at a sanity hearing."

Eliot nodded in appreciation of the truth of this.
"Did—did I even *begin* to put it into words?"

"You simply announced," said the Senator, "that you
had just been struck by an idea that would clear up
this whole mess instantly, beautiful and fairly. And
then you looked up in the tree."

"Um," said Eliot. He pretended to think, then
shrugged. "Whatever it was, it's slipped my mind."

R

Senator Rosewater clapped his speckled old hands. "It
isn't as though we're short of ideas as to how to beat this
thing." He gave his hideous victory grin, patted
McAllister on the knee. "Right?" He reached behind
McAllister, patted the stranger on the back. "Right?"
He was crazy about the stranger. "We've got the greatest
idea man in the world on our side!" He laughed, he
was so happy about all the ideas.

The Senator now extended his arms to Eliot. "But
my boy here, just the way he looks and carries himself
—*there's* our winning argument number one. So trim!
So clean!" The old eyes glittered. "How much weight
has he lost, Doctor?"

"Forty-three pounds."

"Back to fighting weight," the Senator rhapsodized.
"Not a spare ounce on him. And what a tennis game!
Merciless!" He bounced to his feet, did a ramshackle
pantomime of a tennis serve. "Greatest game I ever
saw in my life took place an hour ago, within these
walls. You *killed* him, Eliot!"

"Um." Eliot looked around for a mirror or some
reflecting surface. He had no idea what he looked like.
There was no water in the pool of the fountain. But
there was a little in the birdbath at the center of the
pool, a bitter broth of soot and leaves.

"Didn't you say the man Eliot beat was a tennis
pro?" the Senator asked Dr. Brown.

"Years ago."

"And Eliot *murdered* him! And the fact that the man
is a mental patient wouldn't interfere with his game,
would it?" He didn't wait for an answer. "And then
when Eliot came bounding off the court, victorious, to
shake our hands, I wanted to laugh and cry at the
same time. 'And this is the man,' I said to myself, 'who
has to prove tomorrow that he's not insane! Ha!' "

Eliot, drawing courage from the fact that the four
men watching him were sure he was sane, now stood,
as though to stretch. His real purpose was to bring
himself nearer the birdbath. He took advantage of his
reputation as an athlete, hopped into the dry pool,
did a deep-knee bend, as though working off an excess
of animal spirits. His body did the exercise effortlessly.
He was made of spring steel.

The vigorous movements called Eliot's attention to
something bulky in his hip pocket. He pulled it out,
found that it was a rolled copy of *The American
Investigator*. He unrolled it, half expecting to see Randy
Herald begging to be planted with genius seeds. What
he saw on the cover was his own picture instead. He
was wearing a fire helmet. The picture was a blow-up

from a Fourth of July group photograph of the
Department.

The headline said this:

SANEST MAN IN AMERICA? (SEE INSIDE)

R

Eliot looked inside, while the others engaged each
other in optimistic palaver about the way the hearing
would go next day. Eliot found another picture of
himself in the center spread. It was a blurry one of him
playing tennis on the nut house court.

On the facing page, the gallantly sore-headed little
family of Fred Rosewater seemed to glare at him as he
played. They looked like sharecroppers. Fred had lost a
lot of weight, too. There was a picture of Norman
Mushari, their lawyer. Mushari, now in business for
himself, had acquired a fancy vest and massive gold
watch chain. He was quoted as follows:

"My clients want nothing but their natural and legal
birthright for themselves and their descendents. The
bloated Indiana plutocrats have spent millions and
mobilized powerful friends from coast to coast in
order to deny their cousins their day in court.
The hearing has been delayed seven times for the
flimsiest of reasons, and, meanwhile, within the walls
of a lunatic asylum, Eliot Rosewater plays and plays,
and his henchmen deny loudly that he is insane.

"If my clients lose this case, they will lose their
modest house and average furnishings, their used car,
their child's small sailboat, Fred Rosewater's insurance
policies, their life savings, and thousands borrowed
from a loyal friend. These brave, wholesome, average
Americans have bet everything they have on the
American system of justice, which will not, must not,
cannot let them down."

On Eliot's side of the layout were two pictures of Sylvia. An old one showed her twisting with Peter Lawford in Paris. A brand new one showed her entering a Belgian nunnery, where the rule of silence was observed.

And Eliot might have reflected on this quaint ending and beginning for Sylvia, had he not heard his father address the old stranger affectionately as "Mr. Trout."

R

"Trout!" Eliot exclaimed. He was so startled that he momentarily lost his balance, grabbed the birdbath for support. The birdbath was so precariously balanced on its pedestal that it began to tip. Eliot dropped *The Investigator*, grabbed the birdbath with both hands to keep it from falling. And he saw himself in the water. Looking up at him was an emaciated, feverish, middle-aged boy.

"My God," he thought to himself, "F. Scott Fitzgerald, with one day to live."

R

He was careful not to cry out Trout's name again as he turned around. He understood that this might betray how sick he was, understood that he and Trout had evidently gotten to know each other during all the blackness. Eliot did not recognize him for the simple reason that all of Trout's bookjackets showed him with a beard. The stranger had no beard.

"By God, Eliot," said the Senator, "when you told me to bring Trout here, I told the Doctor you were still crazy. You said Trout could explain the meaning of everything you'd done in Rosewater, even if you couldn't. But I was willing to try anything, and calling him in is the smartest thing I ever did."

"Right," said Eliot, sitting gingerly on the fountain's rim again. He reached behind himself, retrieved *The Investigator*. He rolled it up, noticed the date on it for the first time. He made a calm calculation. Somehow, somewhere, he had lost one year.

R

"You say what Mr. Trout says you should say," ordered the Senator, "and you look the way you look now, and I don't see how we can lose tomorrow."

"Then I will certainly say what Mr. Trout says I should say, and not change one detail of my make-up. I would appreciate, though, a last run-through of what Mr. Trout says I should say."

"It's so simple," said Trout. His voice was rich and deep.

"You two have been over it so many times," said the Senator.

"Even so," said Eliot, "I'd like to hear it one last time."

"Well—" and Trout rubbed his hands, watched the rubbing, "what you did in Rosewater County was far from insane. It was quite possibly the most important social experiment of our time, for it dealt on a very small scale with a problem whose queasy horrors will eventually be made world-wide by the sophistication of machines. The problem is this: How to love people who have no use?

"In time, almost all men and women will become worthless as producers of goods, food, services, and more machines, as sources of practical ideas in the areas of economics, engineering, and probably medicine, too. So—if we can't find reasons and methods for treasuring human beings because they are *human beings*, then we might as well, as has so often been suggested, rub them out."

R

"Americans have long been taught to hate all people
who will not or cannot work, to hate even themselves
for that. We can thank the vanished frontier for that
piece of common-sense cruelty. The time is coming, if
it isn't here now, when it will no longer be common
sense. It will simply be cruel."

"A poor man with gumption can still elevate himself
out of the mire," said the Senator, "and that will
continue to be true a thousand years from now."

"Maybe, maybe," Trout answered gently. "He may
even have so much gumption that his descendents will
live in a Utopia like Pisquontuit, where, I'm sure, the
soul-rot and silliness and torpor and insensitivity are
exactly as horrible as anything epidemic in Rosewater
County. Poverty is a relatively mild disease for even a
very flimsy American soul, but uselessness will kill
strong and weak souls alike, and kill every time.

"We must find a cure."

R

"Your devotion to volunteer fire departments is very
sane, too, Eliot, for they are, when the alarm goes off,
almost the only examples of enthusiastic unselfishness
to be seen in this land. They rush to the rescue of any
human being, and count not the cost. The most
contemptible man in town, should his contemptible
house catch fire, will see his enemies put the fire out.
And, as he pokes through the ashes for remains of his
contemptible possessions, he will be comforted and
pitied by no less than the Fire Chief."

Trout spread his hands. "There we have people
treasuring people as people. It's extremely rare. So from
this we must learn."

R

"By God, you're great!" the Senator said to Trout. "You should have been a public relations man! You could make lockjaw sound good for the community! What was a man with your talents doing in a stamp redemption center?"

"Redeeming stamps," Trout mildly replied.

"Mr. Trout," said Eliot, "what happened to your beard?"

"That was the first thing you asked me."

"Tell me again."

"I was hungry and demoralized. A friend knew of a job. So I shaved off my beard and applied. P.S., I got the job."

"I don't suppose they would have hired you with a beard."

"I would have shaved it off, even if they'd said I could keep it."

"Why?"

"Think of the sacrilege of a Jesus figure redeeming stamps."

R

"I can't get enough of this Trout," the Senator declared.

"Thank you."

"I just wish you'd stop saying you're a socialist. You're not! You're a free-enterpriser!"

"Through no choice of my own, believe me."

Eliot studied the relationship between the two interesting old men. Trout was not offended, as Eliot thought he should have been, by the suggestion that he be an ultimately dishonest man, a press agent. Trout apparently enjoyed the Senator as a vigorous and wholly consistent work of art, was disinclined to dent or tamper with him in any way. And the Senator admired Trout

as a rascal who could rationalize anything, not
understanding that Trout had never tried to tell anything
but the truth.

"What a political platform you could write, Mr.
Trout!"

"Thank you."

"Lawyers think this way, too—figuring out wonderful
explanations for hopeless messes. But somehow, from
them, it never sounds right. From them it always
sounds like the *1812 Overture* played on a kazoo." He
sat back, beamed. "Come on—tell us some of the other
wonderful things Eliot was doing down there when he
was so full of booze."

R

"The court," said McAllister, "is certainly going to
want to know what Eliot *learned* from the experiment."

"Keep away from booze, remember who you are, and
behave accordingly," the Senator roundly declared.
"And don't play God to people, or they will slobber
all over you, take you for everything they can get,
break commandments just for the fun of being forgiven
—and revile you when you are gone."

Eliot couldn't let this pass. "*Revile* me, do they?"

"Oh hell—they love you, they hate you, they cry
about you, they laugh at you, they make up new lies
about you every day. They run around like chickens
with their heads cut off, just as though you really were
God, and one day walked out."

Eliot felt his soul cringe, knew he could never stand
to return to Rosewater County again.

"It seems to me," said Trout, "that the main lesson
Eliot learned is that people can use all the uncritical
love they can get."

"This is *news?*" the Senator raucously inquired.

"It's news that a man was able to *give* that kind of
love over a long period of time. If one man can do it,

perhaps others can do it, too. It means that our hatred
of useless human beings and the cruelties we inflict upon
them for their own good need not be parts of human
nature. Thanks to the example of Eliot Rosewater,
millions upon millions of people may learn to love and
help whomever they see."

Trout glanced from face to face before speaking his
last word on the subject. The last word was: "Joy."

R

"Poo-tee-weet?"
Eliot looked up into the tree again, wondered what
his own ideas about Rosewater County had been, ideas
he had somehow lost up there in the sycamore.

"If only there had been a child—" said the Senator.

"Well, if you *really* want grandchildren," said
McAllister jocularly, "you have something like
fifty-seven to choose from, at the most recent count."

Everybody but Eliot had a good laugh over that.

"What's this about fifty-seven grandchildren?"

"Your progeny, my boy," the Senator chuckled.

"My what?"

"Your wild oats."

Eliot sensed that this was a crucial mystery, risked
showing how sick he was. "I don't understand."

"That's how many women in Rosewater County
claim you're the father of their children."

"This is crazy."

"Of course it is," said the Senator.

Eliot stood, all tensed up. "This is—is impossible!"

"You act as though this was the first time you ever
heard of it," said the Senator, and he gave Dr. Brown
a glance of flickering unease.

Eliot covered his eyes. "I'm sorry, I—I seem to have
drawn a complete blank on this particular subject."

"You're all right, aren't you, boy?"

"Yes." He uncovered his eyes. "I'm fine. There's just

this little gap in my memory—and you can fill it up again. How—how did all these women come to say this thing about me?"

"We can't prove it," said McAllister, "but Mushari has been going around the county, bribing people to say bad things about you. The baby thing started with Mary Moody. One day after Mushari was in town, she announced that you were the father of her twins, Foxcroft and Melody. And that touched off a kind of female mania, apparently—"

Kilgore Trout nodded, appreciating the mania.

"So women all over the county started claiming their children were yours. At least half of them seem to believe it. There's one fifteen-year-old girl down there whose stepfather went to prison for getting her pregnant. Now she claims it was you."

"It isn't true!"

"Of course it isn't, Eliot," said his father. "Calm down, calm down. Mushari won't dare mention it in court. The whole scheme backfired and went out of control for him. It's so obviously a mania, no judge would listen. We ran blood tests on Foxcroft and Melody, and they couldn't possibly be yours. We have no intention of testing the other fifty-six claimants. They can go to hell."

R

"Poo-tee-weet?"

Eliot looked up into the tree, and the memory of all that had happened in the blackness came crashing back—the fight with the bus driver, the straitjacket, the shock treatments, the suicide attempts, all the tennis, all the strategy meetings about the sanity hearing.

And with that mighty inward crash of memories came the idea he had had for settling everything instantly, beautifully, and fairly.

"Tell me—" he said, "do you all swear I'm sane?"

They all swore to that passionately.

"And am I still head of the Foundation? Can I still write checks against its account?"

McAllister told him that he certainly could.

"How's the balance?"

"You haven't spent anything for a year—except for legal fees and what it costs to keep you here, and the three hundred thousand dollars you sent Harvard, and the fifty thousand you gave to Mr. Trout."

"At that, he spent more this year than last year," said the Senator. This was true. Eliot's Rosewater County operation had been cheaper than staying in a sanitarium.

McAllister told Eliot that he had a balance of about three and a half million dollars, and Eliot asked him for a pen and a check. He then wrote a check to his cousin Fred, in the amount of one million dollars.

The Senator and McAllister went through the roof, told him they had already offered a cash settlement to Fred, and that Fred, through his lawyer, had haughtily refused. "They want the whole thing!" said the Senator.

"That's too bad," said Eliot, "because they're going to get this check, and that's all."

"That's for the court to say—and God only knows what the court *will* say," McAllister warned him. "And you never know. You never know."

"If I had a child," said Eliot, "there wouldn't be any point in a hearing, would there? I mean, the child would inherit the Foundation automatically, whether I was crazy or not, and Fred's degree of relationship would be too distant to entitle him to anything?"

"True."

"Even so," said the Senator, "a million dollars is much too much for the Rhode Island pig!"

"How much, then?"

"A hundred thousand is plenty."

So Eliot tore up the check for a million, made out

another for a tenth that much. He looked up, found himself surrounded by awe, for the import of what he had said had now sunk in.

"Eliot—" quavered the Senator, "are you telling us there *is* a child?"

Eliot gave him a Madonna's smile. "Yes."

"Where? By whom?"

Eliot gestured sweetly for their patience. "In time, in time."

"I'm a grandfather!" said the Senator. He tipped back his old head and thanked God.

"Mr. McAllister," said Eliot, "are you duty-bound to carry out any legal missions I may give you, regardless of what my father or anyone else may say to the contrary?"

"As legal counsel of the Foundation, I am."

"Good. I now instruct you to draw up at once papers that will legally acknowledge that every child in Rosewater County said to be mine *is* mine, regardless of blood type. Let them all have full rights of inheritance as my sons and daughters."

"Eliot!"

"Let their names be Rosewater from this moment on. And tell them that their father loves them, no matter what they may turn out to be. And tell them—" Eliot fell silent, raised his tennis racket as though it were a magic wand.

"And tell them," he began again, "to be fruitful and multiply."

A collection of irresistibly funny and wildly imaginative short stories by the author of **Slaughterhouse-Five** . . .

Welcome to the Monkey House

by Kurt Vonnegut, Jr.

Discover the far-out imagination and unique genius of Kurt Vonnegut, Jr. in this long-awaited volume which brings together the finest of the author's shorter works. It is a collection of funny, sad, explosive stories dealing with subjects such as sex, machines, pills, men, women, time past, present and future. The fascinating, fantastic and formidable Vonnegut magic always winds up right on target, an irresistible humor with a superb cutting edge, a storytelling talent that makes reading a pleasure as well as a mind-jolting experience. **Welcome To The Monkey House** displays the enormous range of the author's extraordinary creative vision.

Watch Out: Vonnegut is definitely habit-forming.

"Hilarious, uproarious black-logic . . . a laughing prophet of doom" —The New York Times

"One of the best living American writers." —Graham Greene

"George Orwell, Dr. Caligari and Flash Gordon compounded into one writer . . . In his hands the Silly Putty of contemporary aspirations becomes exploding plastic . . . a zany but moral mod scientist at the controls of a literary time machine . . . he makes his literary instrument sing." —Time Magazine

A DELL BOOK $1.25
ALSO IN A DELTA EDITION $1.95

If you cannot obtain copies of this title from your local bookseller, just send the price (plus 25c per copy for handling and postage) to Dell Books, Post Office Box 1000, Pinebrook, N. J. 07058.